A MISTAKE INCOMPLETE

ALSO BY LORENZO

The Love Fool

A MISTAKE INCOMPLETE

A Novel By
Lorenzo Petruzziello

Published by Magnusmade, www.magnusmade.com

Edited by Lauren Hornberger

Cover design and graphics by hortasar covers
Interior design by Elizabeth Bonadies

ISBN: 978-1735065427

e-ISBN: 978-1735065434

Library of Congress Control Number: 2020919292

First edition

Printed in the United States of America

To a mistake incomplete.
This is not a love story,
but a strong and friendly embrace.
Thank you for inspiring me.

ACKNOWLEDGMENTS

A MISTAKE INCOMPLETE is inspired by noir books and film, both classic and new. I hope to have captured the style, emotion, and intrigue of those stories that I continue to consume. And I must thank my mother for introducing me to classic films. It is through these viewings that I discovered my love for noir.

Thank you to all the readers who picked up my first book, *THE LOVE FOOL,* and enjoyed my first venture into the world of authorship. I was happy to be allowed to take you on a quirky journey through Rome with my characters. And I know you will enjoy these new characters in this neo-noir caper set in Milan.

Thank you to the independent bookshops and to the awesome book clubs that welcomed me with open arms. I look forward to more fun times together with *A MISTAKE INCOMPLETE.*

Thank you to Kelly Whitman for being a meticulous and opinionated beta reader. Without your insights and inquisitive remarks, I would not have improved – what I would call – my most exciting work to date. I appreciate your notes and guesswork taken along your reading journey. And, of course, for laughing with me at my momentary confusion of the words *passed* and *past*.

Thank you to Lauren Hornberger for pointing her editing finger at me, trying to instill grammatical rules, and constantly pointing out my misspelling of the words *from* and *form*. I still blame it on my awesomely quick typing. And I still can't commit to *grey* or *gray*.

Always, of course, thank you to my dear friends and family for the moral support and excitement. Your love sparks the energy for me to continue with this daunting but fulfilling hobby.

Finally, thank you to the people in my life that shared with me their stories of personal afflictions. You've inspired me to include a touch of a deep and important topic into this tale.

With all that said, I thank you all, and thank you a million times, and hope you enjoy the adventure I set for you in *A MISTAKE INCOMPLETE*.

Your magnificent author,

Lorenzo

A Mistake Incomplete

The silence is golden,
I pain you to watch me from there.
Forever emboldened
on similar tracks, then we veer.

Peeks through the windows,
then foggy suspicions, they appear.
A sorrow is broken,
a glimpse to an alternate wager.

A misunderstanding,
or did something or someone interfere?
There's no other reason,
for this blunder unspoken and unclear.

One moment, one window,
and a strong hold to keep,
that embrace in my memory
of our mistake incomplete.

LORENZO PETRUZZIELLO, FEBRUARY 2020

LORENZO PETRUZZIELLO

Chapter 1

Berlin

HIS STEPS WERE careful, and his comfort with darkness allowed him the typical confidence to succeed without a trace. He made his way across the room to the large ornate mirror hanging above an oak cabinet. Lifting the constraining ski mask, he examined his new moustache still coming in. He had decided a while ago that he wanted a distinguished look, and concluded that a moustache should do the trick.

The soft moonlight was not bright enough at this end of the room. To allow him a better examination of his facial hair, he turned on his mini flashlight and shined it onto his face. The moustache was coming in nicely, not too thick, and shaped just perfectly. He looked at the rest of his face, which he tended to do when in front of a mirror – he just couldn't help himself. He noticed that the lighting, positioned as it was at that moment, accentuated his handsome features. Realizing he had distracted himself again, he quickly turned off the flashlight to get back to the matter at hand.

Did he have to put the ski mask back on? What was the point of it? He knew no one was going to see him. And besides, if he was to get spotted on the street or by some neighbor, he thought a black ski mask would definitely call attention to him. He decided it wasn't necessary and kept the ski mask up away from his face. This way, it was easier to make his way around the room.

He was dressed in all black: a tight black shirt with long sleeves and tight, yet flexible, black pants, allowing him agility for climbing over the balcony. His shoes were made of flexible black canvas with black rubber sole. He had perfected this outfit over the years. *Wait*, he thought to himself. *What is that?* He shined the mini flashlight on his shirt. "Is that a fuckin' stain?" he mumbled as he rubbed the white drop. "Where the hell–?" He remembered. "Fuckin' bird."

His gloves were also tight, but their leather made it more difficult to handle objects. He hadn't been able to find his favorite neoprene pair with the metallic tips, which allowed him to use touch screens. Where the fuck had he misplaced those damn gloves? *Damn!* He just remembered. They were in the side pocket of his travel bag in the extra closet in his new apartment. *The travel bag! That's where the other lighter is too!* Flashlight off. He finally turned away from the mirror, aggressively shoving the light back into his small black shoulder sling.

He made his way around the room and took note of the furniture. It was laid out almost exactly as it had been described to him. Bam! He stubbed his left toe on the metal leg of a marble top coffee table. "What the fuck?" he whispered as he lifted his leg and grabbed his toe. It was instinct. That's what one does when one's toe throbs with pain, right? He felt himself fall forward. He tried regaining his balance, but it was too late. Crash! A lamp fell to the floor. It had to have been made of metal because it fell with a multitude of crashes. He fell along with it, but managed to land onto the plush floral sofa. He let go of his leg, realizing he had to get the hell out of there. The floorboards in the ceiling creaked. They were up. The light upstairs had been turned on, illuminating the stairway to the foyer. "Shit." He sprang from the sofa, stepped through the curtains and climbed out of the window from which he had entered.

CHAPTER 2

ONE QUINOA BOWL with vegetables and chicken, and a bottle of cola. The cashier handed him the buzzer with his order number, eight. Stef thanked her in German – he liked practicing this new language and took the opportunity whenever he could. He popped open the bottle of cola with the community bottle opener and then sat at a small table by the window. He had contemplated sitting outside, but the tables sat four and he didn't want to have to be the rude guy that refused anyone from sharing his space. He preferred to eat in peace.

The bright midday sun warmed the Berlin air. It was not too warm. Germany didn't seem to get that stifling heat like the Mediterranean. And that was why he had decided he liked Berlin. The temperature was just right. He felt this way about Copenhagen and Amsterdam as well. In fact, he occasionally tried to make his way up to the northern countries when he could. Granted, he didn't decide on Berlin this time around; the job had taken him there. But he was glad to be there all the same. And the more he made it up to Germany, the more it was growing to be his second favorite – although nothing had beaten Copenhagen yet.

The buzzer vibrated, indicating his bowl was ready at the pick-up station. He dropped it into the metal basket with the other buzzers and took the large quinoa bowl to his seat. As he approached the table, he spotted her: flowing black hair, cascading down the side of a loose and baggy skirt with diagonal fluorescent stripes that met in the middle, creating a V to her knees. Her oversized sunglasses, blue with gold tint, reflected the sunlight into his eyes as she walked by him and into the eatery.

Stef listened closely as she placed her order, took her buzzer, and sat at a table two spots down from him. He kept sneaking peeks at her as she set her sunglasses on the table and dug into her turquoise leather purse. He continued looking over hoping to make some sort of eye contact, but she preoccupied herself with a deep dig until she pulled out a paperback copy of *Pride and Prejudice*. He was in love.

"Anna!" a man at the counter called out, making the woman look up. She locked eyes with Stef and smiled. She placed her red bookmark between the pages, rested the book on the table, and walked over to take her coffee from the counter. Stef wanted to get a conversation started, and had to come up with something. The book. Yes, he'd say something about the book. The woman returned to her seat and picked the book back up again.

"It's one of my favorites," Stef blurted towards her. She didn't respond. Did she even hear him? Maybe she didn't realize he was talking to her...or that his remark was directed at her. He leaned towards her and repeated himself. She looked up.

"Oh, I'm sorry," she smiled. "I didn't realize you were talking to me." Her accent, almost perfect English with a slight hint of German, attracted Stef to her even more.

"Oh, no need to apologize. I'm sorry for interrupting a good read." He pretended to turn back to his bowl, hoping really that she would engage.

"This is probably my seventh time reading it, actually." She closed the book. "I just can't seem to find anything new that compares. I mean, sure it's a basic story we all know, but it's a guaranteed good read. You know what I mean?"

"I do!" He really didn't. He never read the book. "It's just hard to let anything be what it is. I feel like they keep adding too much to stories." He had no idea what he was talking about. So he reverted to some comments someone had made once about a spy film. "Too much action. Too much intrigue. I mean, why can't the story just be the story? Let us take it in. Slowly."

"Yes! Too much is not necessarily a good thing." She picked up her purse. "You mind if I join you?"

Stef tried his best to quietly leave her flat. Anna was fun and exactly what he needed to relieve some pent-up stress. He wanted to get out before she asked him any questions, or worse, asked him to stay. It was easier this way: No awkward *goodbye* or *thank you*. Just leave quietly and forever hold his peace. Besides, he had to get back to his hotel with enough time to shower, check out, and get to the airport.

CHAPTER 3

Milan

WITH ONE EYE closed, she focused on the scissors as she slowly cut a straight line across her fringe. She was always careful when maintaining her bangs. This was her favorite look so far: raven hair, flat and straight, brushed her shoulder as she moved her head while talking or walking. After drying her hair, then a half hour of straightening it with an iron, she stood at the sink looking into the mirror with scissors, polishing the ends of her meticulous home cut.

The fringe was done. Straight, just above her eyebrows, which she had shaped perfectly the night before. She ran her fingers in her hair, making sure it flopped properly with movement. Satisfied, she ran the scissors under the faucet and placed them by the sink to dry.

She then sat at the vintage cream-colored vanity – a gift from one of her interior designer friends – and began her make-up process. The radio in the room was playing pop music from the last decade. She carefully lined her eyelids with a charcoal pencil as she sang along with the male soloist whining about how depressing his nights have been without the girl he thought he loved. Carefully dropping the pencil in the holder before her, she browsed her assortment of lipsticks for the shade of red she was feeling at the moment. The music picked up momentum, inspiring her to grab a hairbrush and croon along with the intense crescendo of the man pleading for the sadness to stop. When she looked in the mirror again, she adjusted the loose wisps of hair, flattening them to perfection.

She looked down again at her collection of lipstick and perused the shades. The tubes in front of her were arranged in shades from bright red to dark espresso. She ran her manicured fingers along them until she saw a color that she felt was right. She was wearing a black outfit, but she wanted her lips to pop. However, she loved the color of her latest acquisition: Espresso Corretto – a mahogany brown that had a hint of red. And it was a matte texture, no need for super glossy lips tonight. She leaned in closer to the mirror and carefully glided the stick across her quasi-Hollywood shaped lips.

Ping! She looked down at her phone and saw it was a message from him – the man she had been messaging with for a couple of months now. They had finally agreed to meet in person. Although she rarely met random men online anymore, she decided this guy was different. His name was Paolo. He had a real job – something about analyzing markets for the retail industry. She wasn't quite sure exactly what he did, but she knew he had an actual job.

She had to admit she wasn't sure if their meeting was an actual date, but based on the way he was flirting with her online, she assumed it was. However, she vowed never to assume – it always led her to awkward situations – so she approached this particular meet-up with caution. That didn't mean she couldn't look her best, though. Just in case.

She opened the message: "Hi there! See you tonight."

"Looking forward to it," she replied with a smile.

CHAPTER 4

SHE ADJUSTED HER thin black wrap, stepping up from the underground station at Moscova stop. Her new strappy shoes already hurt, but it was a sacrifice she was determined to deal with for this night. She found the shoes earlier that afternoon while she browsed the small shops along Corso Ticinese. The pain was starting to happen along the outer side of her feet, but she knew that it would subside as soon as she sat down for dinner. She wasn't expecting to have to stand during the metro ride – which was uncommonly crowded. Maybe a taxi would have been the wiser choice.

At first, she resisted Paolo's offers, but after months of messaging back and forth, she finally agreed to meet him. If it turned out that his intention was to simply hook up, she would be disappointed, but for some reason she was not too offended. He was quite a charmer online. She was used to handling men like that. It had been years, but she occasionally found herself still chatting up a man; however, it was always in person.

Although she preferred not to fall into her past escort-like activities again, she wouldn't say no to this guy, and the guilt consumed her. She had taken herself out of that life years ago. Really, her age forced her to change her ways. She never slept with her clients; it was merely companionship. Most of them just wanted to talk to a pretty woman. And that's what she groomed herself to be: a pretty woman for men to talk to – for a price.

Tonight, she thought they would meet for a simple coffee or cocktail, but she was surprised when he actually suggested dinner. She wanted to counteroffer a coffee date, but decided to take the chance – he seemed really genuine in his messages, and his social media feed appeared the same. So she took the chance and agreed to dinner. When he suggested to meet in the Brera, she felt good about the date – Brera is a safe, well-lit neighborhood. She gave him a time, 19:30, and suggested he pick the restaurant.

Her phone vibrated in her favorite beaded clutch. It was probably him. She clicked it open, pulled out her phone, and read his text: "We're here."

'We'? Who's 'We'? Never in the conversation did he mention others would be joining them. *Maybe this isn't a date? And clearly not even a misunderstood escort situation.* Although it was disappointing, she felt even more safe that there would be others at the table. She could let her guard down now. No need to walk in on the defense in case this guy was a creep. Well, he could still be a creep, but at least others would be there as a sort of shield.

"Be there in 10 min," she replied. She put the phone back in her purse, grabbed a tight hold of her wrap, and picked up her pace. Turning left down via Solferino, she tried to ignore the now unnecessary aches on her feet. *Why did I wear these damn shoes?*

She stepped through the glass door, up the steps into the bright white restaurant. She scanned the few tables on the main floor and spotted Paolo staring at her with a big smile. He was wearing a grey sports jacket complete with a red lapel pin and a pale yellow pocket square. His periwinkle tie lay over a crisp white button down that accentuated his physique. He was seated at a large table of eight. Before she could scan his companions, he jumped out of his seat and rushed up to her.

"Welcome!" He embraced her and added, "Wow, you're really here."

"Yes," she smiled. "It's great to finally meet…"

"Yes, yes. Come. Sit down." He interrupted her and led her around a cream-colored pillar to the far end of the table, by the front window.

They took the two empty seats across from each other. The group of eight people were all dressed exquisitely, all deeply engaged in several different conversations, not noticing their new companion. To Paolo's immediate right was a beautiful woman with a short blonde pixie haircut, wearing an orange top and turquoise earrings that dangled just above her shoulders. The woman was in mid-laugh when Paolo turned to her.

"Elena," Paolo gently touched the woman's shoulder. "Elena, this is Beatrice." Elena's eyes opened wide with excitement, her smile along with them.

"Oh! Beatrice–" She offered her hand. "I apologize. I didn't see you come in."

"Oh, not a problem." Beatrice was still adjusting in her seat as she shook Elena's hand. "Pleasure to meet you." The response was automatic. Beatrice didn't know what to say really. *Who is this woman? Who are these people, and why are they all here tonight?*

"And this here next to you is Charlie," Paolo said as he gestured.

"Hello, Beatrice," Charlie replied while he stood up to shake her hand. She couldn't help but notice his bright blue eyes behind round tortoise glasses. His plum sports coat was accentuated with a pale blue pocket square. He sat back down, accidentally knocking his fork off the table.

"Oh, there you go," Elena laughed. "The husband's away and you have one too many."

"Oh, stop it! This is my first one." Charlie adjusted his seat. "And shut up about my husband." He made a face and laughed into his gin and tonic.

"Here's your fork, Charlie." The man on his left grabbed Charlie's attention.

"Thank you, Antony."

"Nice to meet you…" Antony reached out his arm behind Charlie's back.

"Beatrice." She shook his hand.

"What a lovely name."

"Thank you."

"Beatrice," Elena stepped in, "we took the liberty of ordering for the table. Is that OK or do you prefer to order something specific?"

"Oh, that's great. Thank you."

"Charlie," Paolo chimed in as he adjusted his napkin, "as we were saying earlier, you must get back to Berlin. Elena and I found this amazing little restaurant and immediately thought of you and Elio."

"Yes," Elena continued. "The restaurant is located in a former apothecary and being that Elio is in pharmaceuticals, we thought he would appreciate it. And the food is to die for." The woman on Elena's right showed her something on her cell phone. "Oh, put that away, Silvia. You know it's rude to have that out at the dinner table."

"But it's him," Silvia responded as she put the phone back in her clutch. "He just posted a photo and I wanted you to see it."

"We'll deal with that issue later," Elena replied as she rubbed Silvia's arm, consoling her. "Viviana!" Elena drew her attention to the other end of the table. "I enjoyed your recent article…"

"Elio will be back in a couple of days," Charlie replied to Paolo. "Maybe he and I can pop up there for a weekend."

So many conversations were happening at the table at once. Beatrice didn't know what was going on. Why was she there? What did Paolo tell these people about her? She focused her attention on Paolo sitting across from her, but the confusion of the whole evening was overwhelming.

CHAPTER 5

THE BARTENDER SWIRLED the mixture of gin, vermouth, and Campari in an overly ornate crystal mixing glass. His posture was perfectly straight as he held the rose colored mixing spoon between his fingers and made small circling gestures that forced the ice cubes to swirl and clink. He removed the spoon, letting a drop of the drink fall onto his outer hand. He pressed his lips to the drop, sucked the liquid, and nodded with satisfaction.

He placed the mixing spoon into the small sink to his right, then reached below the counter. He raised his hand to reveal a thick chunk of ice, raised it to the rocks glass that was sitting to the left of the mixing glass, and sized the ice chunk – it was slightly larger than the rim. With his right hand, he grabbed a pick and chipped away at the ice chunk until it was small enough to fit. He then raised the mixing glass and elegantly poured the mixture, allowing it to flow over the ice chunk and hit the sides of the thick glass.

Stef watched the bartender's gaze of serene satisfaction as the red concoction flowed from one vessel into the other. The barman placed the mixing glass into the sink and then proceeded to reach for an orange, which lay in a metal basket to the right of Stef. As the bartender reached, Stef noticed a tattoo on his forearm – a mismatch of nautical creatures outlined in thick black lines stretching from wrist to elbow, and probably beyond. The man grabbed an orange and peeled some of its rind before returning it to the bowl. He turned around and, with a paring knife, cut the rind in the form of a leaf. He then took the leaf-shaped rind with both hands and gave it a slight squeeze over the drink, allowing a small spray of juice to coat the top. Finally, he rubbed the underside of the orange rind along the lip of the glass before dropping it into the ruby red cocktail; then grabbed the glass and walked it over to Stef.

"Your Negroni, sir," he announced with a smirk – or was that a wink? "With our house-made gin."

"Grazie." Stef returned a half smile as the man walked over to another patron at the opposite end of the bar.

"Still up to your old habits, huh?" The voice came from the man to his right, killing Stef's quasi-flirtatious moment. The man sipped his whiskey and continued, "As I was saying, you owe me money."

"Fuck off." Stef rolled his eyes and sipped his rich Negroni. He could feel the man's dead eyes staring at him, but refused to look into them. Instead, Stef kept his on all of the bartenders working on drinks.

"You owe me some money," The man repeated as he swiveled his seat to face Stef, who refused to look.

"That money was for the work I did," Stef responded sternly, hoping to give the man the impression that he wasn't going to be pushed around.

"Yeah, but you came up short."

"I was there." Stef's reply sounded weak, and he knew it. *Shit,* he thought. *Keep up the assertiveness, don't let him intimidate you.*

"Enough of this bullshit." The man tried to whisper, but his words came out stronger than he wanted them to. He continued with a softer tone, "Where's the piece?"

"I told you." Stef kicked up his confidence. Made himself sound like he didn't care. "The piece wasn't there."

"Are you stealing from me? You're not that dumb. You wouldn't take the piece for yourself."

"Are you serious right now?" Stef finally looked at him. The man had a long, thin face with round, green eyes; in between hung a long hook nose. His brows furrowed as he smirked with a malicious grin. Stef turned back to his drink and added, "Fuck off."

The man leaned in. Stef knew it was an intimidation tactic, so he tried hard to pretend it didn't affect him. The man continued, "We got nothing. So, you owe me money."

"That wasn't the deal."

"Stop playing games!" The man slammed his palm on the bar.

Fortunately, the music was loud enough to cover the sound of it. When Stef looked at the man again, he gently took his hand off the bar as if he realized he could have been noticed. Stef looked at his drink again and replied.

"I don't play games. That money was a deposit – for the risk."

"You failed." The man's voice was harsh.

"Then you're lucky." Stef was glad he got a rise out of him. It was the moment he knew playing it cool kept him on top. "You don't owe me the rest."

"I want my God damn money back." The voice spilled through his teeth.

"You paid for my services."

"Not rendered."

"Listen." Stef had had enough. He turned to the man and slammed his finger down on each point. "I was there. I climbed that damn wall. Onto that balcony. And I crawled into that fucking window. That was what you paid for." As he said these last words, he jabbed his finger into the man's chest.

The man looked at the finger, then up at Stef. The tables had turned back. The man was now on top.

"Yeah," the man replied with a softer tone. He knew he had the upper hand. "Well, we got nothing in return. And we don't like that."

Stef was angry. He turned back to his drink. "Life's tough, buddy. Get used to it." He took a hard sip and slammed his glass down.

"Ready for another?" The bartender appeared again looking down at Stef's glass. "Or are you still working on that?"

"Hi. Uh…no." Stef was surprised to see the bartender leaning on the bar with both hands, staring into his eyes with such intensity. Stef added, "I mean, I'm still working on this. Thanks."

"No problem. Just give me a wave when you're ready." The barman straightened up, threw a red bar towel over his shoulder, and walked away.

"I sure will. Thank you." Stef smiled at him and then realized his companion was still there watching him. "You still here?"

"I'm not leaving without my money."

"Well…" Stef was flustered. "I don't have it." He held his drink up in front of his face, looked at it, and sipped.

"That's very bad, Stef. Very bad." The man slowly got up off his seat.

"Where are you going?" Stef was definitely flustered.

"Relax, man. Just going to have a cigarette. You want one?"

"Listen, Flavio…" Stef took a drag from his cigarette. "Don't get your panties in a bunch. Just throw me another job, and I'll waive the deposit."

"Ha! Now, why would I hire a clumsy joke of a thief like you again?"

"That's not fair, man." Stef flicked some ashes to the ground.

"Do you know what they say about you?"

"No. And I don't give a fuck."

"Face it, Stef. You're finished."

"Oh, what's this now? You're not going to send someone? Are you doing your own dirty work?"

"I don't like to get my hands dirty. You know that."

Stef took a long drag of his cigarette, blew a puff of smoke toward Flavio's face , and replied, "Fuck You."

"I'll be back for my money," Flavio replied. He threw his cigarette in a puddle and stepped onto the street.

"Another job!" Stef called out to him.

"We'll see," the man replied, then leaned in close and added, "You should quit this shit. You're still not good at it. And the cigarettes? I can smell you from a mile away." Flavio knocked Stef's cigarette out of his hand and walked away.

CHAPTER 6

THE WHOLE SITUATION was overwhelming for Beatrice. She had finally accepted that the night was not a potential romantic connection – and she was confused as to why Paolo had made it appear so. She sat at the table trying to include herself in one of the several conversations, deciding to take the night as it was: an evening out with new people and a gourmet meal. Paolo kept talking over her, mansplaining and responding to questions for her. She decided he was not for her anyway, so she ignored his antics and focused on the delicious food instead.

Granted, she could have just left. But why bother? She trudged all the way down to the area with the most painful shoes, and she wasn't going to let this asshole ruin her night. Who knows, maybe she'd meet new friends? The main point was that she was hungry…but really, she was curious to know what the hell this was all about. Why did Paolo even invite her out tonight? Maybe he wasn't expecting this crowd. Maybe he was planning to cheat on Elena. It was clear they were together. And if that was the case, why had he been messaging with her? What did he expect was going to happen tonight? She didn't care anymore.

The servers removed the appetizers and returned with the next course. They elegantly placed the dishes before each dinner guest, encouraging them all to enjoy. Beatrice admired the presentation of the plate before her. The golden yellow risotto Milanese – the classic saffron dish with bits of osso buco laid out in a straight line across the plate.

"Stef!" Veronica called out to the man just entering the restaurant. The name brought back memories. Could it be him? Beatrice wasn't sure, but she hoped it was. What were the odds of finding an old acquaintance at this awkward dinner?

"Ciao tutti. Scusa del ritardo." Stef went around the table kissing and hugging everyone until he got to Beatrice. They locked eyes. Did he recognize her? She couldn't tell. She smiled at him, but still no recognition came from him.

"Oh! Stef, this is Beatrice." Elena was clearly the connector of the group. "Beatrice, this is the ever-so-mysterious Stef."

"Mysterious?" Stef replied, looking back at Elena.

"Well, we didn't know if you were going to join us or…"

"I'm always there for you, Elena, you know it." He looked back at Beatrice and offered her a hug. "Nice to meet you, Beatrice," After pulling away, he looked her over again with a quizzical look. "Have we met before?"

"I'm…"

"She's new to the group, Stef," Paolo chimed in. Beatrice wanted to slap him.

"Oh, well, welcome," Stef replied and walked to the other end of the table.

"Thank you." Beatrice sat back down, avoiding eye contact with Paolo. She was done with his shit. Instead, she watched Stef finally make his way to the empty seat next to Silvia, probably still trying to remember where he had met her. That was the moment Beatrice again appreciated her painful strappy shoes.

CHAPTER 7

AT ELENA'S DIRECTION, the group walked down the street to enjoy a post-dinner cocktail. Fortunately, the sky had stopped teasing rainfall, instead providing a drifting fog.

Beatrice had intended to leave the dinner immediately after dessert, but she was determined to talk to Stef. He must have remembered her. Well, maybe. Did he not remember her? Or maybe he was covering it up? Did he really not recognize her? She had to find out.

"Beatrice," Paolo called out from behind her. "Did you enjoy the dinner? I'm glad you joined."

"What?" She barely paid attention to him. Instead, she was focused on Elena catching up to Stef ahead of them.

"Are you heading home?" Paolo continued.

"Home? What? Why would I head home? I thought we were moving on to a bar?"

"Oh!" Paolo appeared nervous with her response. "I just assumed…"

"Assumed what, Paolo? Assumed that you put me in an awkward situation?"

"What? Whatever do you mean?"

"Why did you invite me tonight?"

"Uh…"

"No, why were you even contacting me? What the hell was this all about?"

"I like you."

"Stop. Don't." She put her hand up. "I don't care. We're done. Leave me alone." She broke away and continued to follow the troupe as it turned the corner. From the back of the group, she watched Elena make her way to Stef, but she couldn't hear what was being said.

"Will I see you tonight?" Elena whispered with a smile. She clearly wanted to avoid anyone overhearing.

"Elena, don't do this. Not now." Stef laughed aloud pretending Elena had said a joke.

"Oh, please. Paolo can't hear us." She gave him a slight jab on his arm. She turned from Stef and drifted toward her sad friend. "Silvia! Dai…sbrigati…"

When the group reached the bar, Elena exchanged a few words to the doorman, who immediately hugged her and made way for them to enter.

The bar was located by Porta Nuova, on the ground floor of a small hotel. Every wall was a window to the street, with the exception of the back wall, which was covered in greenery and had a doorway that led to the hotel lobby. The bar, shaped as a square in the middle of the room, was decorated with brass bars along the edge. It was surrounded by plants with large fan-like leaves, giving the whole place an appearance of a birdcage in a jungle.

The hostess pointed to a small section of plush mauve velvet seats and small, round brass tables set aside for Elena and her group. Beatrice found Stef alone at the bar. This was her moment.

"OK, I have to confess now," she said as she took the seat next to him.

"Oh, hello. Confess?" Stef's facial expression changed to false pleasantry with his reply. He was clearly in a moment of thought that Beatrice had interrupted.

"Yes. You don't recognize me?"

"Recognize you? So, we have met before?" He replied with a genuine smile, but his head was trying to compute where he had met her. *Shit! Was this a date that went bad? Or maybe a former client? Who was she?*

"Yes, Stef! Look closer. Think…"

He looked her face over and something was familiar, but he couldn't place it. He thinks he had slept with her, it must have been a long time ago. "Interestingly, when I met you in the restaurant, I thought I recognized you, but…How do we know each other?"

"OK, you've got to be kidding me." Beatrice put her head on his shoulder and added, "Stef, think Rome…"

"Wait a minute…the Cin Cin?"

/ / /

She hadn't thought of the Cin Cin bar since she left Rome years ago. That was where she had first met Stef. She was working at the bar, located in a small corner of Trastevere. Stef had come in a couple of times to visit her coworker Patrizia. Beatrice was enamored upon their first encounter. So enamored, in fact, that one of the times he had come in to see her coworker – who happened not to be there that evening – Beatrice ended up in his bed.

/ / /

"Wait. Hold on." Stef looked her face over. "Your hair, it's different."

"Well, I have been changing my hair a lot. Patrizia taught me that it's a way to refresh one's life. I've decided to embrace my real color again. I was tired of the alias. It made me feel like a criminal. And besides, who was I really hiding from? My parents? Please."

/ / /

Beatrice had come to Rome as a student from the United States. She had completed a year-long study abroad program, and decided she wasn't going back, much to her parents' disapproval. In doing so, she had overstayed her student visa and had been living and working under the table ever since.

/ / /

"Well, based on what we've done, one could assume we were in hiding," Stef replied with a chuckle.

"Well, those were different times...we were younger and foolish. I don't engage in that stuff anymore. It's dangerous."

/ / /

They had spent two months together hiding from Patrizia, who had no idea the two had been sleeping together while the women were living under the same roof. Eventually, Stef realized Beatrice had many boyfriends – she had referred to them as clients – although she vowed she rarely slept with any of them. They only wanted her companionship, and they paid a hefty price for it. She wasn't even shocked when she found out Stef was a thief and dabbled in a similar line of work.

/ / /

"You're quiet." Beatrice looked his face over, trying to read his thoughts. "I suppose you still steal or see people?"

"Sometimes." His confession was somewhat embarrassing. But he felt relieved to be able to talk about it with someone. "It's just different now. Had to change the strategy, new clientele. But it doesn't bring in as much as it used to."

"Stef! Wow...I mean, you need to move on. We're not that young anymore. They want the young ones, not us."

"Wow! I can't believe it's you. How long has it been? When did you come back to Europe?"

"I never left actually."

"What?"

"I decided to just not go back. That's when I changed my life. As a waitresses I got paid under the table...and besides, I was getting more and more from the *side gig*."

"Yeah, OK, but after we parted ways..."

"You mean after you abandoned me?"

"Oh, come on. I was with Patrizia." Stef stopped himself and looked down. "I came back for her, you know. And found her with that stupid American. I couldn't watch. I had to go. You know that."

"Yeah, I know. Sometimes, I wish I followed you."

"It was actually smart of you not to. I got into a lot of trouble. I could have gone down a really bad path. Fortunately, I was smart enough to keep up my appearances...that's how I found this group."

"You mean one of these people hired you?"

"No, no...I met the group at some art opening here in Milan. My plan was to rob them, but I realized they were introducing me to all these potential marks, that I should keep them around."

"So, that's your gig now? Thievery?"

"Shh...no. I mean, sometimes. Well, it's complicated."

"Isn't it always?" She shifted in her seat, looking back at the group, making sure no one was approaching.

"What were you doing here tonight?" Stef reached for her arm, softly grasping it as he spoke. "How did you meet these people?"

"I don't know any of them, actually." His touch was like lightning. All of the attraction was relit. She wanted him. Again.

"I don't understand." He kept his hand on her soft forearm, gently rubbing the bone on her wrist.

"When I came to dinner tonight, I wasn't expecting a crowd," she responded. His touch was irresistible. She remembered their moments in bed. She wanted him again.

"What were you—Wait a minute." Stef removed his hand and sat back, looking at her. "Was someone here a potential customer? You are still in the shit, too?"

"No. No. God, no. I told you, I no longer engage in that…OK, well sometimes opportunities are presented, but I don't always take them."

"So, who hired you tonight?" he said with a smirk. He looked back at the group, trying to sort it out.

"No one."

"Paolo. It was Paolo, wasn't it?" He looked at her. She didn't look away.

"Not really," she replied without conviction. "I mean, he didn't *hire* me, really. I think we were meeting to see…"

"See what?"

"Well, honestly – and I'm embarrassed to say this, but it's you, so I'll tell you – I thought this was going to be a date."

"With Paolo? Ha!"

"Why not?"

"He's with Elena. He'll never leave Elena. No one would ever be so dumb as to do that."

"Why not?"

"It's Elena, that's why. Elena is everything. She's everyone. She's the nucleus of the group. The glue that ties everyone together. It's just her way. Everyone loves her."

"Well, I can see what you're talking about. She is quite fascinating."

"Fascinating is an understatement. She's just Elena."

"Well, Paolo is no longer my interest anyway." She leaned on the bar, rubbing her right ear. "Especially after putting me in that situation. I had no idea what was going on or what to do or not do. Say or not say. I wanted to get up and leave. In fact, I was planning to leave just after dinner."

"Why didn't you?"

"Because you showed up. I mean, what were the odds we would see each other again? Like that? I couldn't wait to talk to you."

"Well, it is a nice surprise. A great escape from all of this."

"Escape?"

"Sometimes I just want to let my guard down, you know. Let loose. It's nice to talk to you. You understand my past. And you don't judge it. These guys would never understand. I miss you."

Beatrice woke with a start. Stef was propped up on his right arm, poking her shoulder.

"Beatrice. I'm sorry to wake you, but…and I hate to ask this of you, but…"

"What's wrong?"

"You have to go."

"What?!" She was shocked and insulted.

"I'm really sorry, but someone's on their way over and…"

"Oh my god. You…you have clients come here?" She was disgusted, suddenly feeling dirty, thinking of the strange women that shared the pillow and the blankets that covered her. She quickly sat up, kicking herself out of the bed.

"Beatrice, relax."

She struggled to pull up her dress, searching for her fucking painful shoes – which she wanted to throw at him.

"Beatrice, what are you doing?"

"Never have I felt so cheap…"

"What are you talking about?"

"What do you take me for? What the fuck have I done? How did I fall for this again? I'm so stupid."

"Beatrice, what are you going on about?"

"I'm just gonna go." She left the room.

"Wait!" Stef jumped up after her, meeting her at the foyer door. "Beatrice…what's going on?"

"You've got a client coming here. You…you…I wish I never…" She turned the doorknob.

"Beatrice, don't go like that."

"Like what?"

"Angry…there's really nothing to be angry about. I think you misunderstand."

"Misunderstand?"

"Yeah…I mean, first of all, I never bring a client here. In fact, there haven't been those clients in a very long time."

"Then who's coming here?"

"It doesn't matter. But it's not that."

Beatrice narrowed her eyes. "Is it Elena?"

"What?"

"Never mind, I'm leaving." She opened the door and walked out, ignoring his beckoning, instead focusing on the loud clunks her shitty shoes made as she quickly hobbled down the wide stone steps and out of the building.

Chapter 8

HE SHOWERED AND dressed, and tried not to think about how he may have hurt Beatrice. He didn't want to tell her where he was going nor with whom he was meeting. He thought it best to keep this particular side hustle to himself. Even though he was glad to have Beatrice back in his life – someone he would be able to talk to about this other side of him – his aversion to trust had won the battle.

It seemed like half of Milan had decided to take up jogging in Parco Sempione that morning. Stef walked around the perimeter of the park to the Triennale's Palazzo dell'Arte. He looked up at the building and recalled Elena describing it to him on one of their afternoon strolls. *The palazzo was designed by Giuseppe Muzio...it opened in 1933, which started the tri-annual design fair known as the Triennale...*

He entered the museum and immediately looked to the right, where the Italian Design exhibition was permanently held. He spotted the typewriter designed by Olivetti – remembering Elena excitedly pointing to it as she had once guided him through the exhibit. He walked into the room and spiraled into reminiscing about the day Elena had taken him there. But he quickly reminded himself that he probably could never have a relationship with her.

He stared at the Grillo telephone of the 1960s, a chair by Magistretti, and the arching lamp by Achille Castiglioni. He remembered Elena pointing to other creations by design studios Ponti and Memphis Milano. He most remembered her excitement for anything made by her idol and preferred designer and architect Gae Aulenti.

Stef snapped out of the depressing excursion and continued through the building to the garden café in back.

"So, you've calmed down and come to your senses?" Flavio folded the newspaper and looked at Stef, who had just joined him.

"Let's do this. I'll finish your fucking job. When?" Stef pulled in his metal chair, noticed the server approaching. "Un caffe, per favore," he called out before the server approached. The server nodded and walked away.

"Next week," Flavio continued. "Thursday night. The place will be empty this time."

"Yeah, about that...there wasn't supposed to be someone in there that first night."

"No, there wasn't. And we had no idea someone was home. It was unexpected."

"What? And no apology?" Stef replied, and then thanked the server who had placed the coffee in front of him.

"Do you want this job or not?" Flavio continued as soon as the server had left.

"Yes. Let's get this shit over with and you out of my hair."

"Well, you know all the details. You've got your flight. Get it done."

CHAPTER 9

WALKING BACK FROM the park, Stef still had to remind himself to go in the opposite direction. He had relocated recently, and the move was an emotional one. When he had first unpacked in his new space, he realized the downsizing restrained him from having all of his beautiful stuff around. Instead, he was surrounded by boxes of those material things with which he refused to part.

His gorgeous, extra-large former living space was taken from him. He couldn't afford to keep up with the expenses. The elite Brera neighborhood, where he had prided himself on living, was almost no longer his home.

He had two options: He was forced to either take a smaller space or move to a different quarter altogether. He didn't think he could handle living outside of the Brera, so he opted for the smaller space. OK, maybe that was a slight exaggeration on his part, but he had to keep up appearances, try to get back into and maintain the lifestyle to which he had grown accustomed.

He had thought maybe taking up some of Flavio's low-level theft jobs would have helped, but he managed to fuck up that first and very simple one in Berlin. That screw-up was a hard reminder that he was out of practice.

He was too old to be doing petty cat burglary. *Fuck Flavio and his bullshit jobs anyway*, he kept telling himself. He had to find another solution that would provide larger results. He had to get himself back on top. But when he attempted to step back into his other former income flow – companionship for money – it only reminded him that he was passing his prime. His vanity made it difficult for him to accept that he had already passed it. The realization had hit him hard.

As he continued on to his new apartment with trepidation, he thought about that very moment he first felt old. It happened only recently.

/ / /

He had heard about a new cocktail bar that opened up near Porta Romana. The bar was all the buzz underground, not yet mainstream knowledge. Therefore, the clientele were either people in the know or friends of friends that had the privilege to access this discreet locale. This was important to Stef because he knew full well that such clientele would be the perfect prey for his advances. He knew he still had the looks, but was his age showing yet? He wasn't sure.

Getting into this place wouldn't be a problem for Stef – after all, he knew the bar scene very well, and he was connected to Elena. He had worn his best new sports jacket – flashy yellow with a thin black basket weave pattern. The color created enough pop to invite glances, and they always looked at Stef.

He left the first two buttons of his crisp, white shirt unfastened, exposing his smooth neck – another invite for glances. Stef knew that an exposed neck was a turn-on. The voyeur would imagine her, or his, lips pecking all over it at the start, during, and sometimes after the engagement. He would get in the mood just thinking about being desired. He liked feeling desired. He liked taunting the onlookers. He wanted them to look, and he would do anything to keep their attention.

He had hoped his night would be a success. No, he was confident it would be. There was always someone out there looking for a good time. So, even if no paying clients could be found, there would always be someone up for just fooling around.

With one last glance in the mirror, he went out into the living room. The floor in there cracked even louder than the one in his bedroom. Although it was a beautiful marque wood floor, every step creaked like a haunted house. And with every creak, he reassured himself it was only temporary. Every time he looked down at the floor, he discovered a new crack – well, new to him. He counted the cracks and creaks and…was that a tear in his eye? He stopped and composed himself. His determination to get a paying client tonight grew even stronger. He grabbed his keys and calmly sauntered out the old, heavy door.

He stepped out of the building and remembered to turn on his charming smile. *Always look like you've got it together*, he told himself. *Always.* The apartment building was located at the very end of a dead end street. He stepped onto the narrow sidewalk, avoiding the cracks and holes in the dilapidated street. He hoped no one would ever discover where he now lived. But should it ever come up, he already had his story: He had purchased a new space, but it was going through remodeling – to his liking – and the apartment he was in now was a temporary space he was crashing in while his friend was out of town. *What friend? Who cares? A friend you don't know.*

Taxi? No. Tram. He had a public transport pass, so the tram would be a more economical route. That was the first moment he thought of economics. He never had to think of money – well, not to the extent of deciding between a taxi or tram. Was he poor? No! This would be resolved. A tram would be interesting, though. Maybe a space to meet more potential clients, he had convinced himself.

Shit. What tram would he have to take? He didn't remember. He stopped at the corner of the main street and pulled out his phone. He punched in the bar's address and selected 'Directions'. Mode of transportation: Public. Metro…Tram. Tram 19. OK, where to get that particular tram…There's a stand at Piazza della Repubblica. Done. As he put the phone back in his pocket, he turned left and looked at the taxi stand ahead of him. He walked past the waiting taxis and crossed the street towards the tram stop. Was that another tear in his eye?

Shit, is this too far? His stop may have been two stops prior, but Stef had been lost in his shame. How did he let himself get back into this financial situation? Is this what they mean when someone says they're having a breakdown? Stef pushed the stop indicator as the tram approached Porta Romana. Oh well. He convinced himself not to let the little things push him to a breaking point.

He knew the place was somewhere in the neighborhood. He shouldn't have a problem finding it. He needed to go to via Crema. *Focus, Stef.* He walked a few blocks back to via Crema and sought via Monte Nero, where he located the small blinking blue and pink neon light that indicated the entrance to the locale.

The front entrance was a tiny room with a white counter along the left wall. The walls were papered with blue and black satin flower designs, like something from Marie Antoinette's dark closet. A narrow white door was the focal point of the back wall. To its right hung a small oval painting of a woman with a head of a grey cat, dressed in a Louis XIV era gown, holding a fan and a white mask. Above the door was a blue neon light in the shape of an arrow pointing left. A pink neon arrow hung to the door's left, pointing up.

On the counter lay three black rotary telephones and a small white sign held by a clip. On the sign, written in calligraphy, were the words *Ascolta il tuo destino.* Stef had no idea which telephone to select. He just went for the phone on the far left, put the horn to his ear, and listened to two cartoon-like voices conversing about clothing. He returned the horn and selected the middle telephone. On the other end of the receiver were sounds of grunting and a hoarse voice eventually asking for condoms. Stef rolled his eyes and picked up the final telephone, but all he could hear was the crackling sound of static. As he listened to the white noise, a group of three well-dressed women came in from the street. They smiled at Stef, walked past him, and opened the narrow, white door. Stef watched them stroll into the bar. The last girl to enter looked back and laughed at him as she shut the door. What a fool. Stef shook his head, dropped the receiver, and opened the door for himself.

Just as he reached for the handle, the door opened. Muffled ambient music spilled out as a slender, bearded man in suspenders exited the private area and shut the door behind him. Stef did not recognize the man, but it had never been a problem to get into exclusive places before. However, as much as he hated to admit it, it was Elena who was the key to entry every time. She knew everyone and never had a problem getting into places. Stef had taken advantage of that over the years. He had forgotten the difficulty in passing the barriers.

He had to play it cool, as if he belonged. He brushed past the slender man, attempting to reach for the handle again. But this time, the man's arm blocked him.

"I'm sorry, sir, but this is a private club. Members only."

"Very funny. I'm sure I'm on the list: Orso, Stefano."

The man reviewed his tablet with stern eyes and a smirk. He looked up again. "Again, sir. You're not on the list. May I escort you out?"

Stef was tempted to drop Elena's name, but he didn't want her to find out what he was up to. He just stared at the man, squinted his eyes and gave a flirtatious smile. The man smiled back. Stef had always been able to count on his charm. The man then lowered the tablet and said, "This way to the exit, sir." Stef was shocked. Never had he failed at seducing door people. What was happening?

"No, that's not necessary," he snapped. Defeated, he exited the bar and went for a walk to cool off.

What to do now? Hotel bar. Hotel bars were always an easy target for Stef. But which hotel should he target? How embarrassing that he could not get into that private club. This was not right; something was off. *It's my age,* he thought. *It's noticeable.* Age was peeling away his keys to entry. Would he be able to even get a client tonight?

It was finally occurring to him that he was out of practice and rusty at the hunt. It had been many years since he relied on selling himself for income. Since making connections with wealthy people – thanks to Elena – he figured out swindling money was somewhat more respectable. It wasn't until that night that he realized the companion thing had never been this difficult for him before. He needed to come up with a strategy. The stumbling along the way bullshit was not working for him.

CHAPTER 10

STEF LAY IN bed alone, not sleeping a wink. The thought of having to do the job in Berlin again was eating at him all night. When he tried to get his mind off of that, the argument with Beatrice took over. It was a night of one shitty thought after another. Eventually, his mind drifted to that awful night years ago in Rome.

/ / /

Stef had slipped in through the back door and waited in the kitchen for one of them to appear. The door to the bar opened, causing the 60s music to slide in with a woman in a pink bob wig. It was Beatrice. The neon lights reflected off her metallic green miniskirt. She slid the door shut behind her and dropped the tray onto the counter, not noticing that Stef was standing in the back doorway watching her.

"You look fantastic," his voice appeared from the shadows.

She put her hand to her heart and realized it was Stef.

"My goodness, Stef!" She ran to him, put her arms around him, and gave him a full, deep kiss. "I love to see you."

Stef kissed her back, pulling her into him and up against the back wall. He raised her skirt from behind, but she quickly slapped his hands away. He tried raising her shirt, and she slapped his hands away again. He continued kissing her, then pulled away.

"What's wrong?" she pleaded.

"Is she here tonight?"

"Yes, but you already knew that." Beatrice pulled away and adjusted her shirt, defeated. She walked over to the mirror and fixed the blue feather clipped to her pink wig.

Stef walked over to the kitchen door's window and peeked through to the dancefloor. He spotted Patrizia in a slinky, silver dress and a platinum white wig with a long green feather.

"You need to let her know." Beatrice's words were like daggers to his heart. "We have to tell her."

He ignored Beatrice and opened the door to the main room. Patrizia was at the center of the floor attempting to dance the Charleston with some guests. Stef snuck up behind her, put his hands on her waist, and pulled her down into the oversized chair just behind them. She fell into his lap and laughed as he pecked her on the cheek.

"Let's get out of here," he whispered in her ear.

Patrizia laughed, embraced him, and gave him a kiss.

"I want to talk to you," he continued.

"I can't right now," Patrizia replied. She peeled his arms off of her and stood up. "I'm working. You know that."

"I want to see you," he pleaded.

"Stef, we've already talked about this," Patrizia said as he followed her behind the bar.

"Just give me one more chance."

"Stef–" She didn't finish her sentence. One of the servers, with a red mask hanging from his neck, had come to the bar with a drink order. Stef watched as Patrizia's eyes lit up following the server's path to a group of Americans.

"Patrizia."

"I can't right now." Patrizia's gaze broke from the patrons back to him. "You have to go."

"Can we see each other later?"

"No," she replied curtly. "I need some time."

"Where is he?" Stef refused to go without her agreeing to see the man he knew she was looking for. "Is he here? Is this why you won't talk to me?"

"Stef," Patrizia rolled her eyes. "Just go. We'll talk later."

Stef turned away, defeated. He returned to the oversized chair and dropped down, watching Patrizia.

"You have to let it go," Beatrice asserted from behind the chair.

"Why?"

"She's over it." Beatrice walked around and wiped the small white table in front of him. "She's got her eyes on someone else."

"Is he here?" Stef sat up. "Beatrice, has she really found someone else? Where is he?"

"Yes, he's here," Beatrice replied with a hint of satisfaction. It was as if the idea of his and Patrizia's relationship ending was an opportunity for her to step in. Stef couldn't let that happen. Sure, Beatrice was hard to resist, but he wanted it to work with Patrizia.

"Which one is he?"

"He's over there, by the statue."

Stef followed her nod to a sculpture of two lovers embracing. To its right was a couple sitting on a blue couch.

"That couple?"

"Well, this is the first time he has come in with *her*." Beatrice crouched down next to Stef. "But he has also been in with some beautiful tall blonde."

"I don't understand."

"He's been in here with other women," Beatrice explained as she leaned on the chair's arm. "But Patrizia seems to enjoy him very much. They spent some time together."

The words pained Stef. He couldn't think of Patrizia with someone else. He wanted her to be with him, and only him. Although he had his work, he was always devoted to holding onto a monogamous relationship. Patrizia was that for him, and he didn't want to let her go. He hoped she would come around.

"Do you think she'll come back to me?"

"Stef," Beatrice said, "you have to just let it go. She's not comfortable with the whole situation. When she found out about you, she was hurt. I had to stay with her all night to comfort her. She had no idea what you were, what you did."

"I was going to tell her at some point."

"No, you weren't." Beatrice sat down on the ottoman next to him. "You were trying to end the work. You thought you could just sweep it away and she wouldn't ever find out."

"How did she find out, Beatrice?"

Beatrice shook her head in disgust, stood up, and walked away.

"Beatrice—" Stef followed her into the kitchen. "Beatrice, you told her, didn't you?"

"Stef…" Beatrice wouldn't look him in the eyes. She kept her focus on emptying the dishwasher. "Stef, you must understand."

"Understand what? That you sabotaged our relationship?"

"What?!" Beatrice dropped the hot utensils onto the metal counter. "Are you kidding me right now? You don't get to be the victim here, asshole. You know it wasn't right what you did. She really liked you, and you kept ignoring her. And you are such a complete dick that you fell into *my* bed."

"Why did you take me to your bed?"

Beatrice rushed up to him and slapped him across his left cheek.

"Get out of here. Get out of our lives."

"Beatrice…"

"Just go." She pushed him to the back door. "Go away. You fooled me. You fooled her. We're done with you. Go."

"But…"

"Go!" Beatrice shouted at him and slammed the door shut.

/ / /

That night was the first time he had realized that Patrizia knew about Beatrice and Beatrice knew about Patrizia. That the two had talked about Stef with each other.

And now, Beatrice was angry with him again. His rush to get her out of his apartment probably reminded her of that time in Rome, that time he played both of them. He had to make it right with Beatrice. He had to apologize to her, again.

CHAPTER 11

THE CHICKEN STOCK simmered in a small, yellow pot on low flame. It was what Beatrice had in her pantry, but she knew she could make it work. She diced an onion while listening to one of her favorite heartbreaking love songs coming from a small speaker to her left. Although the tear in her eye was not from the onion, she deceived herself that it was.

She added the diced tearjerkers into a wide, steel casserole pan, their sizzle announcing that the cooking had officially begun. She sprinkled a pinch of salt and watched the onion sauté until translucent – her cue to pour the dried rice into the pan. She gave the mix one or two stirs and proceeded to stare into the pan as she listened to the deep voice of the Italian crooner singing pleas to the woman he had just met, telling her that he just knew he was already in love. *The same whiney crooner and he's still delusional.*

As the rice toasted in the pan, she remembered she had forgotten to grab the saffron. She rushed over to the pantry and rifled through her spices. Thankfully, there was a container of saffron, enough for one recipe. Relieved, she placed the red strands in a tiny glass bowl and added some of the warm chicken stock. She set it aside for later. The rice was now translucent, ready for the wine bath. She poured a dry white wine into the pan, enough to just cover the rice. Sizzling, the alcohol cooked off into a steam that Beatrice used to open up her pores as if she had a kitchen culinary spa. She waved her head above the pan, letting the aromatic vapors caress her face.

What is he going on about? The singer passionately droned on about his weakness from this instant and delusional love. Beatrice had had enough. She forcefully tapped the radio screen and changed to a classic rock station, convinced the songs would be less about heartache. Immediately, the drums and guitar riff boosted her mood. As Freddie Mercury sang about another one biting the dust, Beatrice danced around the island counter top, almost forgetting her risotto simmering next to her.

She rushed over to the pan. The rice soaked up almost all of the wine as it bubbled. It was time to start adding the stock. Beatrice tightened her apron, grabbed one of the ladles from the utensil holder, and added three scoops to the casserole pan. As the liquid simmered, she danced some more.

Her phone pinged with another text. How many times would she have to ignore his texts before he got the hint? She looked away from her phone, poured the saffron infused stock from the small glass bowl, and gave the rice a little stir. She continued with a couple more ladles of stock, ignoring what was most likely another sad attempt at an apology. *Fuck off, Stef.*

Again, the phone rang. If it was not multiple texts, it was the calling. She rolled her eyes in frustration and reached for the phone. Reluctantly, she accepted the call on speaker while she continued working on her now bright orange-yellow risotto.

"What do you want?"

"Beatrice, please let me in."

"There's no need. Go home."

"I want to talk to you. There's a misunderstanding."

"Misunderstanding?" She slammed the wooden spoon on the counter. "Stef, yes there is a misunderstanding. You misunderstand how foolish you made me look again. How you made me feel. It's over between us. I'm not doing this again. Leave me alone."

"Beatrice, don't say that."

"Stop calling me."

"Beatrice…"

His voice was charming. It was as if he knew his saying her name made her weak. She wanted to open that door and ravage him. But she kept her cool.

"I need some time away from you," she said. "Please just stop."

"I'm at your door. Please open. Let's talk this through."

"Go away."

"Where do you want me to go? No, don't answer that."

"Oh, I don't know…why don't you find a new client. Or, no wait – go to Elena? Go be her side dish. That's clearly what you prefer."

"Beatrice…" Stef replied more calmly. "Please open the door."

"Leave." She tried ignoring Stef's knocks, but each one hit her heart like a hammer to a nail.

She composed herself, adding the final ladle of stock to her risotto and watching it simmer. Under the sounds of an unhinged guitar riff, the knocking had ceased. She listened closely, soon finding herself sobbing over the bright yellow rice.

Chapter 12

BEATRICE WAS IN a daze as she tidied up behind the bar. The place was closed for the night, but sitting at the other end of the counter was her final patron: a handsome man who had been drinking in the same spot most of the night. He was a slow sipper, and he swayed in his seat, very drunk and very quiet. Beatrice continued to clean up when her concentration was interrupted by the sound of an empty glass banging on the wood. The drunk patron had accidentally tipped it over while attempting to wave for her attention, asking for another drink. She rolled her eyes and pursed her lips.

"Sir, we're closed," she reminded him again.

"Oh, how about just a shot of whiskey, then." The man struggled to get his words out as he pleaded.

"Do you need me to call you a taxi?" she insisted.

The man shook his head, put his finger up, and turned to slide off the stool. Instead, he stumbled off, but managed to steady himself onto the bar.

"S-s-sorry," he slurred and pointed to the restroom, signaling a request for permission to use the facilities.

Beatrice nodded frustratingly. At least it was some progress to get the man out of the place. She watched him as he stumbled to the restroom, closing the door behind him. Knock, knock. Stef stood at the window in the front door with puppy dog eyes, pleading to be let in. She took a deep breath and walked over to the door. She wanted to tell him to screw, but unlocked the latch instead. Maybe he could be useful in getting the drunk patron to go.

"I'm really sorry for…" Stef immediately burst in.

"Don't. Just don't." Beatrice closed the latch behind him. She walked past him as he took a seat.

"Are you almost done?" he asked. "Wanna go for a walk?"

"I've got someone here still," she replied. "He's in the restroom. I just want to get home."

She wiped down the counter, put the man's empty glasses in the dishwasher, switched it on, and proceeded to wash the utensils sitting in the sink. When complete, she dropped the rag.

"Would you mind keeping an eye on him when he comes out? Try to make him leave." She pulled a cigarette from under the counter. "I'm going to step out for a smoke." Without waiting for his response, she unlocked the front door and stepped out, leaving Stef at the counter. She didn't want to be near him. A cigarette was her great escape.

When Beatrice returned, she found Stef behind the counter, sweating profusely and nervously swigging from a bottle of whiskey. He looked at her with complete worry. Something was wrong. Beatrice was confused.

"What's with you?" she asked smiling, half joking, as if asking the question in a light manner would make his response a joke, but it wasn't.

Stef kept silent, looking at her, then at the restroom door, then back at her. She followed his eyes and quickened her steps towards him.

"Stef, are you OK? What's wrong?" She put her hands on his arms and looked at him.

Stef lowered the bottle of whiskey and dropped his head onto her chest.

"He's dead!" he cried.

"Dead? What are you talking about?" She grabbed him by the hair and lifted his head off her chest. "What happened?" She didn't wait for him to answer. She pushed him aside and rushed to the bathroom.

Underneath the white marble sink, she found the man laying down on his left side. She took a deep breath and put her hand to her mouth in shock. He was facing down on the floor facing the wall. Blood dripped from a small gash on his forehead. *What happened to him? How did it happen? Did he bang his head on something? Did I give him too much to drink? Was the floor wet? Did he slip? The sink? No. Maybe?* She didn't know. She was trembling. The police. She had to get them involved. There was no way around it. She had to contact the police.

"What are you doing?!" Stef shouted when he saw the phone in Beatrice's hand. "Who are you calling? No! Stop. Put the phone down. Stop for a minute, please."

"What are you about, Stef? I have to call the police." She struggled to shake a cigarette out of the pack. She set the phone down, picked up the lighter, and lit the cigarette set in her trembling lips. She blew out the first puff of smoke, set the lighter down, and picked up the phone again. "What am I supposed to do?"

"Just wait." Stef walked over to her, gently taking the phone from her trembling hands. "Let's just think this through a bit."

"Think this through?" She tried to grab the phone from Stef and failed. "What's there to think about? There's a man on the floor in the bathroom. Dead."

"Shh. Shh. Shh…" Stef put his finger to Beatrice's lips. "Let's just calm down, breathe, and sort this out."

"Stef…" Her response was muffled by his finger again.

"Beatrice," he continued in a soft tone. She loved it when he said her name. It relaxed her. She pulled away and took another drag, which also helped calm her. "Let's figure out the best way to handle this," Stef continued. "Think about it for a minute: We are the only ones here; you and I. Which makes us the prime suspects to whatever happened to that guy in there."

"Wait a minute." She looked up at him. The words he just spoke hit her in a different way now. She was upset. "You were the only one in here."

Stef looked away and stepped back behind the bar, reached for the whiskey, and took another swig. She followed him and continued.

"I was outside having a cigarette," she exclaimed. "You were here alone with him."

"No, I wasn't," Stef replied in between swigs. "I was out here, waiting for him to come out."

"Stef!" she said his name as if chastising him. *Why would he do anything like that? It's not like him.* She persisted, "What did you do?"

"I heard a noise," Stef ignored her implication and continued, "and went back there to check on him. And I found him on the floor."

"Was he already dead when you found him?"

"What?!" Stef couldn't believe she asked him that question. "Of course he was! What do you take me for? Have you ever known me to be a murderer? I occasionally thieve, Beatrice, but I'm not a murderer. You know that!"

It was true. She did know Stef was not a killer. He was too much of a coward to kill anyone. She looked at him in his state of anxiousness. He looked very handsome, sweating and worried. She sat on the bar stool and finished her cigarette.

"Stef, I have to call the police." She reached for the phone, still in his hand. "You know I do."

"Beatrice, you can't call the police. You know you can't. We can't get involved with the police."

"You mean *you* can't get involved with the police."

"You can't either, may I remind you. Do you keep forgetting your situation, and your past?"

"They won't care I'm here illegally. Will they? And as far as that other thing you're referring to, that was cleared up. And you know it." She hopped off her seat and rushed behind the bar. "It was a one-time offense, and besides, in the end there was no proof that man was paying me. The police let it go. It was cleared."

"Was it, Beatrice? Was it really?" Stef moved back to the other end of the bar holding the phone up in the air, away from her reach.

"Why are you doing this?" She was jumping to reach the phone. "Stef, please don't do this. We don't want any trouble. You or me. We need to do the right thing. Please hand me the phone."

"Beatrice, please stop and think." Stef was relieved she had stepped back. "While it is true that I definitely do not want the police around me – I can't have the police around me, especially now – you have to remember that you can't get involved in all that either." Stef could see that she was listening and understanding. "Beatrice," he continued. "Sure, you cleared up your history. You managed to get all of that behind you. You've gotten yourself out of the escort business."

"I was not an escort," she protested. Sure, she accepted money for companionship, but she never slept with her clients – never. She was a beautiful, young woman who was offered grand things for a date. That was all it ever was. And if a man wanted more, she knew how to get out of the situation; and fortunately, she always did. Sometimes, it was with the help of Stef – the one man who knew her secret life. The secret life that drew them together back in Rome. Drew them to have a secret affair behind her friend Patrizia's back. Drew her to betray her friend for him.

"Do you remember back in the day?" Stef interrupted her thoughts. "We had it good, Beatrice, really good. You were getting cash and gifts…we were living a great life in our twenties." He slowly got closer, embraced her, and continued: "They know us, Beatrice. They have files on us."

"They have a file on you," she retorted, to which he cocked his head and looked at her like a parent silently reminding the child they weren't fooling anyone.

"They'll know where we came from, our past, and where we are," Stef continued. "They won't believe us. We'll be dragged through the slow, arduous process of an investigation. And I fear they will give up and find a way to pin this on us. We can't get involved in this, and you know it."

"Stef…" Beatrice dropped her head on his chest and cried. "Stef, that's not fair. We never did anything bad; not like this. I thought it was over. I thought leaving Rome and coming here would have put that all behind me. I got this new life…I'm doing just fine."

"I know, love," Stef cooed as he rubbed the back of her head. "I know. Unfortunately, no matter how hard one tries, the past still finds its way back. Sure, we didn't do anything awful, but it's all they need to make us suspects. They will see us as the seedy people they want to get rid of."

"Don't ever mention that ever again!" Beatrice shouted. "I've been out of that shady business for years." She repeated it as if assuring herself she was fine. She lifted her head, stepped out from behind the counter, and reached for another cigarette. "It's you, Stef. You have more to lose here than I. You are the one who is still in that life of stealing and conning and whatever you do. You're only looking out for yourself here, not me."

"Hey, hold on. I'm not a con man. Beatrice, you can't call the police," Stef pleaded. "Please don't call the police."

"What do you expect me to do here?" She struggled looking for her lighter. Where did she place it? "You want me to let you go? Give you a head start? You would leave me here to deal with all this? Alone?"

"No! No. No…" Truthfully, Stef had already been thinking exactly what she said. But because she caught on, he knew he couldn't do it. He kept forgetting how intuitive she was, especially when it came to anything he was up to. He had been so used to fooling people, he forgot how difficult it was to coerce her – the woman who knew him all too well.

"Well, what do you expect me to do here?"

"Beatrice…" He knew she loved it when he repeated her name. He joined her on the other side of the counter. Standing behind her, he whispered, "Beatrice, we're in this together." He wanted to reel her in. "It's you and I again. Just like back in the day, in Rome. I've got your back, and you've got mine. No matter what happens, it's you and me. Just you and me."

Beatrice turned around to face him. Their faces were close enough to kiss. She looked in his beautiful eyes, followed his sharp nose down to his cupid-like lips. She couldn't lose him. She didn't think she could do this without him. She knew it.

"What do you propose we do, then?" she whispered.

"Beatrice." His lips gently brushed hers as he spoke. Relieved that he succeeded in hooking her, he blurted, "I'll get a car. We'll clean this up. We'll move him."

At the sound of his words, she couldn't help the feeling of guilt. She knew she would look back at this moment as the turning point, the moment she had conceded to help alter the situation. The moment she had agreed to be his accomplice to whatever idea he had in mind. She knew it was not the right thing to do, but she trusted that Stef knew what he was talking about – and she didn't know why. Was her revived infatuation clouding her judgement? Maybe. But at that moment, she wanted to prevent the past from coming back, and to survive the situation, with Stef.

The other feeling that bothered her was the worry about whether Stef would really return with a car and not leave her behind.

Chapter 13

IT TOOK A while for Stef to find the right car. It had been years since he had resorted to stealing a vehicle. He had moved on from that low-life form of robbery. His expertise had advanced to more valuable items like art, jewelry, or passports. Taking a vehicle was beneath him, but this whole situation was unlike him anyway; and stealing the car fit the crime. Why was his life going backwards? He had moved on from all of this.

His plan: Put the body in the trunk and drive the car to a seedy part of town. But he didn't know yet how he wanted to dispose of the evidence. He could roll the car into the canal, but he decided getting it further out of the city would probably be best. He would drive it out of town. He could, maybe, light it on fire. He'd make that call when he had to, and depending on the resources he could get his hands on. For the moment, he focused on quietly backing the car into the alley behind the bar.

He pulled the brake handle to stop the car, and then popped open the trunk and rang the back doorbell. When Beatrice opened the door, Stef was met by her worried face.

"Are you OK?" he asked as he propped the door open with a loose brick that the bar owners use for deliveries.

"Yes," she breathed heavily. "I was freaking myself out there for a sec, but glad you're back. I couldn't find a tarp or anything, but I did find a large blanket."

"No, it's probably best that we don't use anything that belongs to the bar. We can't have anything tracing back here. Nothing." Stef reached into the trunk. "I pulled this from a construction site." He held up a plastic tarp and bungie cords. "The cords belong to this car."

"What are we doing?" she asked almost in general, but really wanting to know his plan.

"We wrap him up in this." Stef folded the tarp under his arm. "And we drive over to a lake or maybe a river and drop him in the water."

"And the car?"

"Well, initially I thought we'd leave him in the trunk and roll the car in the water, but then I realized the car would be easier to discover, which would lead to the quick discovery of the body. If we separate the two, there's less of a chance to connect the car and the body, and the bar, and us." All of that came to Stef in an instant. He hadn't thought about that until she asked. He was impressed at how quickly he had come up with the plan.

Beatrice followed him back inside. "Wait!" She stopped, kicked the brick that was propping open the door, and closed the lock. "We can't have anyone popping in. You never know."

"Hmm…" Stef was impressed. "I hadn't thought of that. Good work. Now, let's wrap him up."

They went into the bathroom to assess the space and what needed to be done. It was a small room, not enough space to maneuver.

"Should we pull him out there? Then wrap him?" Beatrice suggested but stopped herself. "Wait. No. We can't make more of a mess than there is."

"I'll just need some help rolling him in this." Stef laid the plastic on the bathroom floor next to the man. "And we'll seal it shut with these cords. Then it will be easier to carry him out to the car, I hope."

"He's pretty thin," Beatrice added. "I think we can handle it." She still couldn't believe what she was about to do. She held the tarp in place while Stef rolled the body onto it. He wouldn't touch the body. He used part of the tarp to handle it and shift it on its back, then on to its right side. The tarp was small, not allowing them to cover the whole body. They folded the right side of it onto the torso, partially covering the man's face. His face! Beatrice stared at him. He looked like he was asleep.

Stef nudged her to help roll him up like a rug for transport. He tucked the bottom corner onto the man's feet, while Beatrice struggled to cover the gash on his sleepy face. They stretched three bungie cords around the roll, fastening them tightly. All that was left were the small spots of blood on the floor.

"I mixed bleach in that bucket over there." Beatrice pointed to the corner by Stef. "Let me have the brush."

Stef handed her the brush, and Beatrice scrubbed the blood – which, to both of their surprise, easily wiped clean. When the blood was gone, Beatrice flushed the water down the drain in the center of the room.

"I'll be right back." Stef stepped out and returned with a linen cloth he had also found in the car. "Dry it up with this."

"OK," Stef walked over to the upper portion of the body. "I'll take this side. You take the feet. And we'll carry it to the car. If it gets too heavy, let me know and we'll stop."

"Wait–" Beatrice ran out to the back door and propped it open again with the brick. "OK."

They carried the wrapped body out of the bar and dropped it haphazardly into the trunk. Fortunately, the scrawny man really was light as a feather. Stef slammed the trunk closed and looked at Beatrice. They stood in the dark, staring at each other as if making a silent pact. They were really doing it. There was no turning back from their decision. They were in it together. And no one was to ever know about it. They went back into the bar, closed all the doors, and turned off the lights.

"Wait," Beatrice stopped. "I have to leave from the front door. I have to set the alarm and lock up from the front. I'll lock you out in back. Meet me out front."

"No," Stef held her arm. "I don't want the car to stop out front. Meet me around the corner. I'll give you five minutes."

It was now three in the morning. They had been driving for almost an hour. Stef wasn't sure where to stop. He had originally thought to stop just outside of the city, plop the body in the canal, and continue on to discard the car. But in a sense of panic, he continued to drive.

"Where are we going?" Beatrice asked between drags of her cigarette.

"I don't know yet." Stef kept looking in the rear view. "But we need to end this soon. Before anyone notices the car missing. And especially before anyone notices the man missing."

"The canal was a bad idea," Beatrice suggested. "God forbid the body float into the Navigli. I want it gone. Away from here. Away from us."

"I know. I know. But we can't be caught with this stolen car. We have to get rid of both, and now."

The upcoming highway sign said Lago Iseo. Stef took the exit.

"The lake." Beatrice read his mind. "OK, that may work. I still can't believe we're doing this."

"Beatrice," Stef kept his tone calm and reassuring. "Like I said, we both can't have this on us. The police were on my tail last year, and it took me a while to shake them off. All these guys need to do is read my files and put me under suspicion."

"But you didn't do anything." Beatrice said it, but still felt unsure. "Right, Stef? You didn't do anything?"

"Right." Stef gave her a serious look as if to tell her to trust him.

"Well, I didn't do anything either. So why would they assume we did anything?"

"We were the only ones there, Beatrice. You know how all that shit works. Even if they don't find any evidence, they'll put us under the microscope. They'll read my files, and they'll pull up yours."

"It was just one time," Beatrice rationalized. "For that one time they arrested me with that man – which, by the way, was all on him; I just happened to be in the wrong place. They can't put me in jail for that now." She looked around the car. "But for this…for this we could be done for."

"No one will know. Trust me."

CHAPTER 14

HE AWOKE IN a burst. He struggled to breathe. His mind swirled, as if fighting its way to maintain balance. Were his eyes open? He couldn't see a thing. Darkness. What was that noise? A sudden jostle. He was moving. Was he in a vehicle? Where was he? He took deep breaths, and still struggled. He realized some sort of plastic fabric was covering his face. He tried reaching up to move it; maybe it was how he was laying, but he found it difficult to turn. In fact, it was quite a struggle to move at all. He squirmed until he was able to turn his head up and free his mouth from the plastic on his face, and breathed.

Another jostle. He was in a vehicle. He felt he was moving. Another bump. Where was he? What happened? The last thing he recalled was drinking at a bar. He went to the bathroom and… all he remembered then was this very moment, waking in this state.

He was laying on his left side. He tried moving again, then realized his hands were constrained. Something was wrapped around him, holding his arms in place. He looked around in the darkness. His eyes seemed to have adjusted, but his head was still spinning. Every now and then he caught a glimpse of red light, giving him a chance to see the tight space, and finally realized he was in the trunk of a car. What the hell was happening? How did he get in there? Why was he tied up? Who did this to him?

He squirmed more aggressively until his arms could get some movement. He managed to free his forearms, upper arms still constrained. He felt a rope or something around him. Maybe he could wiggle it up enough to allow his arms to reach up and unfasten the constraint. He steadied his legs against something – he didn't know what – and wiggled his upper body until whatever was binding him made its way up, freeing his elbows.

Suddenly, a clicking sound with a faint flash of yellow-orange light brightened the space. The driver had turned on the directional. With this new light, he saw how small the space really was. The hood of the trunk was directly in front of his face. What the hell was he doing in the trunk of a car? He had to free himself. He frantically ran his fingers along whatever it was that held him – it was a bungee cord. He felt the clasp, which with one move he was able to easily unfasten. Arms now free. The plastic had been wrapped around him. He unraveled it from around his face and body, and took many deep, slow breaths.

The vehicle was slowing down. He listened. Was that music? Whomever was driving was listening to the radio. Did he hear voices? Was there more than one? Who were they? That was irrelevant. He thought he should kick and scream until they let him out. However, it was probably better to take his captors by surprise.

He had to figure his way out of this situation. He felt around him for anything with which he could defend himself. A box. A case? It felt like maybe an emergency kit. As he tried opening it, his elbow slammed against a metal piece behind him. He kicked at the wall of the trunk as he felt a rush of pain along his arm. The car slammed to a complete stop. He lay still listening. Did they hear him? He could hear muffled voices.

"…are you doing? What happened?" Was that a woman's voice? No response. At least not one he could hear. After a minute or so, the car moved again.

He concentrated on the voices, but all was muffled over the sound of the moving car. His head still groggy, spinning over and over, he closed his eyes. Darkness.

CHAPTER 15

THE CAR CONTINUED on the windy road towards Cremona. Stef didn't know why he had changed his mind and chose to go towards Cremona, instead. The Po River popped in his head, and he had no idea where on the Po to go. He wanted to drive into a big town so as to avoid any attention. But he then decided a small, dark area would probably be best. He looked for a sign pointing to a small village.

"Remember those days, Beatrice?" He put his hand on her thigh. "Remember how good we had it? Living the life. Making cash, hand over fist. And how easy it was. Your beautiful looks and my handsome physique; people threw money at us just to spend time with them. Oh, it was so easy."

"Yes, but you slept with your clients. I didn't." She knew it was harsh. She wished she didn't say it.

"Well, sometimes things escalate," he smiled. "Things just happened. And why do you always make a point to clarify what you hadn't done?"

"Right," Beatrice replied with a feeling of hurt and jealousy, ignoring his question. The old feelings she had ever since she found out years ago that he was sleeping with his clients.

"Awe, don't be like that, Beatrice." Stef could sense her emotion. He rubbed her thigh. "You know you were the one I wanted to be with; all the time. I'm sorry I hurt you. You know that, right? I still want you. I always will."

"Don't start with that again." Beatrice inconspicuously wiped the tear from her cheek. She didn't want Stef to see she still had those feelings for him. She felt his hand moving up her inner thigh. Although she was enjoying the feeling, she grabbed his arm and moved it away.

"You know," Stef said in a more serious tone, "once in a while, I look in the mirror and I'm reminded how looks fade. I mean, I know I'm still an attractive man, but I don't look the same. It's not as easy anymore. Hasn't been for a while."

"Ha! Ha! You *are* still trying to keep up the work. Ha! Ha! I thought you moved on to thievery?"

"Don't laugh at me. You're one to talk."

"I don't want to get back in that mess. I get offers still. They are a little different though, but I still get offers."

"Different?" Stef replied, teasing her. "How different? I'm sure they're after the same thing they were back then. They just think you'll give it up easier at your age."

"Fuck off, Stef." Beatrice hit him on the arm. "What I was talking about was marriage. They are proposing marriage."

"Guys say anything for it, and you know it."

Stef turned off the main road onto a narrow one which led them to a bushy meadow on the riverbank. He pulled the car onto the stones by the water, pulled the brake, turned off the car, and popped open the trunk.

CHAPTER 16

THE BODY APPEARED to have shifted. How did the wrap come off of it? Stef also noticed the bungie cord had come undone.

"That explains it," he said while refastening the cord.

They grabbed the wrapped body – limp but still warm – and shuffled across the rocks to the water. Stef let Beatrice put her side of the body down into the water as he slowly pushed the rest of it deeper into the river. The man sank halfway but floated back towards them, the wrap coming undone as it bobbed in the still water.

"We should have brought a weight." Stef looked around for large rocks. "Help me get that stone over there. We've got to throw it on top of him so he goes down."

"But you want him here? Wouldn't you want him deeper in the river?"

"We don't have time to get a boat."

"Fine," Beatrice threw her hands up in defeat. "Let him be then."

Stef placed his foot on the body's head and gave it a long, hard push, sending it further out into the river.

They drove away and stopped in a seedy area outside of Cremona. The sun was beginning to come up.

"We should roll this into the water too or something," Stef suggested. "To get rid of any fingerprints or anything. I mean, I'd prefer to light it up, but that would cause…"

"Over there," Beatrice pointed to a junk yard. "Let's just drop it there."

"I want to get rid of anything that traces the car to us."

"Well, how are you going to do that?"

"In the water," Stef replied as he drove up to the edge of a ditch that led to another part of the river. "We'll just put it in neutral and push the thing in."

Beatrice looked around for any belongings that may have dropped out of her purse. Stef watched as she shifted in her seat making sure she hadn't dropped anything that would incriminate her. Beatrice looked up and noticed him staring at her with a smirk. He turned off the car and put his arm on her headrest.

"So," he shifted in his seat. "Wanna fuck?"

"That isn't funny, Stef." Beatrice rolled her eyes, got out of the car, and slammed the door shut. She had to get out of the car. She found herself drawn to him again. He was so crass, but something about his desire made her want him. She remembered when they had first met in Rome years ago.

Stef was quite the charmer back then, and apparently still managed to be that charmer. Everything always came easy to him; he had the looks, the personality, and an air of mystery – no one really knew what he did for a living. He was smart. He rarely spoke about his work. Once in a while he would drop a mention of this or that, sort of alluding to sales, but he was always vague enough for anyone inquiring to fill in the blanks.

Oh, he was good. Very good. So good that his vulgar request in the car had not insulted her as much as she wanted it to. She couldn't shake being attracted to him. The feeling she got from just knowing he was interested in her made her feel guilty and foolish. She had to step out of the car, just to keep this awful task moving forward. She could not believe she let herself be a part of it. What was she thinking?

Stef met her behind the car and they pushed the vehicle, letting it roll down the ditch and into the river.

They walked to the town's central train station and bought the first ticket for the morning commuter train into Milan.

They blended in with the early morning crowd going into the city for a day's work. Stef sat with his leg propped on the seat in front of him, while Beatrice nervously devoured half of a chocolate covered *colomba* panettone she had picked up at the station's coffee bar. He smiled at her.

"What?" She asked with her mouth full, in mid chew and half shame.

"You have chocolate all over your face," He replied with a smirk, then closed his eyes until he felt her poking his arm.

"Come on," she said. "This is our stop. I need to get to the bar. I don't even remember if I finished the usual clean-up for the next guy today."

"Aw, I don't want to go back there," Stef replied as he followed her off the train. "I thought we could go to bed. And if we were up for it, you know…"

"Stef! Can you focus please? After what we've just been through, I think we need to make sure to – as you kept saying – cover our tracks."

"Fine, fine," he replied with a yawn. "Then we can fuck?" To which he received a forceful slap.

CHAPTER 17

"YOU COULDN'T HAVE gone at the train station?" Beatrice struggled to fit the key in the bar's front door lock. With the door finally open, she punched in the alarm code.

"You know I can't go in those dirty bathrooms." Stef pushed passed her. "Sorry, I really have to go!" He ran to the bathroom where the body had been just the night before.

He tried ignoring the image of it as he rushed to the urinal, unzipped, and relieved himself. He breathed out, and stood still picturing the body in his mind. Finally, he zipped up and walked over to the sink under which he had discovered the man. He quickly washed his hands, wanting to rush out of that bathroom.

Beatrice switched on the one light behind the bar and looked things over. She freaked at the empty stool where the man had been drinking that evening. It was a reminder that what she and Stef had just done really did happen. She was trembling again. What had she done? She heard the toilet flushing, surprised at how sounds seem amplified when the bar was empty. She turned on the faucet in the sink and washed her hands. As the water rushed over her fingers, she couldn't help but cry. What had she done? Who was that man? Someone out there must be looking for him, waiting for him to come home.

She opened the dishwasher. Were they already cleaned? She couldn't remember, so she ran the load again. She grabbed a towel and cleaner to wipe down the whole bar. She started with the area where the man sat. She pictured the man waving his glass for a second round. She stepped in a puddle. It wasn't any color, really. It looked like it could have been vodka or Sambuca maybe. Did she ever give him that shot he requested? How much had he spilled? It was more than a shot of liquor on the floor. Was it water? She pulled out the stool. More liquid. What had he spilled? Then she saw something laying on the floor, and screamed.

"Beatrice!" Stef ran out to her. "What is it? Are you OK? Beatrice…"

She was trembling again. She stood still, staring at the object and ignoring Stef.

"Beatrice," Stef embraced her. "Beatrice, what is it?" He followed her eyes and saw what she was staring at. It was a brown leather wallet, lying flat and wet in a pool of water.

"Stef," she cried into his chest. "How? Who? Is he…?"

"Calm down, Beatrice." Stef slowly pushed her away and bent down to look closely. "He could have dropped it before he went into the bathroom."

"Why is it wet? Where did all this water come from?"

"Relax." Stef reached under the adjacent stool and picked up a broken water bottle. He stood up. "We need to get rid of it."

"Don't touch it!" She held his arm.

Stef shook her off, reached over the bar for a long mixing spoon, and bent back down to prod at the wallet. He slid the spoon between the crevice of the wallet and lifted the object up onto the counter.

"It's heavy." He laid the wallet open on the bar. "It's soaked." He tried to pull out the identification, but the spoon wasn't doing the job. "Do you have tongs?"

"Soaked," she repeated as if in a hypnotic state. "How can it be soaked?"

"Tongs, Beatrice. Let's focus."

She went behind the bar and found the small utensil she used for garnishing drinks. She raised it up. Stef nodded and put out his hand. Beatrice slowly put the tongs in his hand, trembling again as she did it. *Soaked.* The word ran through her mind as she did it.

"Why is it soaked, Stef?"

"I don't know," he replied as he concentrated on pulling out the identification. The ID card was from the U.S. The name on it: Kevin Benton. Chicago, Illinois. "Kevin…"

"Do you know him?" She shook with anticipation. "Stef, who is he?"

"I don't…no idea…" Stef tried placing the name, but he had never heard it. "No matter, Bea. We need to dispose of this."

"What? How? Where?"

"I'll take it. We'll drop it in the canal."

"What if someone finds it?"

"If someone finds it, they find it. It's just another lost wallet."

Beatrice was not completely sold on the idea, but had no other choice. She gave Stef a half nod, hoping it would be the end of all of it.

"Come on." Stef grabbed a cloth napkin from the table on his right. He wrapped the wallet in it, folding the cloth snugly on all sides. "Are you done here? Let's go for a walk."

Beatrice threw the tongs and cloth in the sink and set the alarm before locking the door behind them.

CHAPTER 18

HIS FACE WAS wet. Why was he soaked? Had it rained? Did he fall? He found himself on a bank, half of him in water, the plastic tarp still attached to his left leg. He was groggy and in pain, everything around him spinning. It was dawn.

He propped himself on his elbows and crawled out of the water onto the rocks. Finally able to untangle the plastic from his leg, he had no idea what happened. He remembered the car, the voices; prior to that, it was all a blur. He lay down on the rocks, trying to adjust his eyes from the spinning, when headlights lit up the shrubbery to the left.

He heard car doors open and saw lights flashing on the water. Two men walked along the bank, eventually making their way towards the rocks. The lights blinded him, and as the forceful arms lifted him up, he found blackness again.

CHAPTER 19

Berlin

HE WANTED TO slow down, catch his breath, but he knew he had to keep moving. He rarely ran. In fact, he hated it. But when one is almost caught breaking into a house, one has to run like there is no tomorrow, and Stef ran his little heart out.

That fucking Flavio set him up again. He was told no one would be home. He should have been able to just climb up the balcony and back into that living room, retrieve the wooden box, and leave. But, again, someone was home. This time, quick on their toes, the person called the police.

The person didn't see Stef jump out of the window and off the balcony and run down the street into the night. Stef was sure of it, but he didn't want to take any chances. He fled on foot. After running for forty minutes, he dashed into a park, lay in the bushes, and breathed. He rested on the grass, staring at the stars, feeling the failure once again. No wooden case. Another failed attempt at burglary. Maybe because his concentration was overtaken by that awful night with Beatrice. He still couldn't believe they did what they did. But no police had come around. No one seemed to have found a body. The car was probably found, but no connection to anything. He was safe. They were safe.

Why did he leave Beatrice for this Berlin job? He was too old for this shit. He was done.

CHAPTER 20

HE AWOKE WITH a start. He was breathing heavy and sweating, haunted by what they had done. It was another restless night lost to his thoughts. When Stef had gone to bed, he could barely keep his eyes open, but as soon as he had rested his head on the pillow, his mind had started spinning again.

What had he done? That whole situation at the bar. That body. What the hell possessed him to do all that? To get Beatrice to go along with it? How selfish was he? He hadn't even thought about the position he had put her in. And now what did she think of him, leaving her for this stupid Berlin job? Another failure. Nothing positive was on his mind.

He managed to doze off in small increments, but failed at getting a deep, full night's sleep. With every burst of waking, he reached for his watch on the nightstand to his left. Finally, at 4:15 in the morning, he decided it was his threshold of fully waking up or attempt to doze some more. He really had no reason to rush. He had no plans other than catch his flight to Paris that afternoon. From there, he was instructed to catch a train to Milan – it was, as Flavio explained, a way to avoid any direct connection.

Stef remembered rolling his eyes at the whole idea, but he went along with it anyway.

He continued to just lay there, failing to fall asleep, but he knew there was no point. He decided to just start the day.

He ripped the covers to one side, propped himself on his right elbow, and looked out the window. Below a dark sky, city lights glowed on the buildings before him. A thin glow of sunlight outlined the skyline, giving him the final rationale that his day could probably begin. This was the time to do a yoga routine or some sort of cardio maybe. He would try it. Yoga seemed less strenuous than a full on run. Run? He hated running. And after last night, he proved to himself that running was not for him. Why had that even crossed his mind?

Yoga. Calming stretches would force him to close his eyes and take deep breaths, starting a new day in a chill mindset. And the feeling of participating in some sort of healthy routine would indeed boost his mood. But first, he had to pee.

He rolled out of the bed. Without turning on any lights, he shuffled into the bathroom, kicked up the toilet seat, and relieved himself. Standing there, half asleep, one eye closed, he yawned so strong that he released a long, drawn out whine. Three shakes and a flush. Done.

He moved to the sink, turned on the faucet, and finally looked up. The mirror – a window to devastating truths. He stared at his silhouette, the soft glow from the partial sunrise allowing his reflection to come into focus. The shadows covered more of him, and he saw the man he had remembered. The man he missed. The man he was still looking for. The man whose prime lingered longer than most men. His handsome looks made life easy for him. He didn't know what it meant to try very hard – he never really had to.

He was desired, and he knew it. He had learned early on how to capitalize on his treasure and used it to his advantage in every area of life. But he knew that once he turned on all the lights, he would see the man he was now. He would look at his real reflection and ask, "What the fuck happened to you?"

He ignored the reality of that reflection in the mirror. He wouldn't look at it long enough to see something new. Like those awful droopy eyes. He began his usual routine of washing his face with a charcoal deep cleanser. He looked in the mirror again, as if for the first time in a while, and this time he noticed his eyebrows were a disaster. Looking closer, he noticed a few curly, dead strands wildly flowing through his thick, short, brown head of hair. It was time for a good trim. He almost didn't even pay attention to the small bags under his eyes – he preferred to ignore that they even existed – but knew the morning face cleanse was a must. "What the fuck?" The nose hairs creeping out of his nostrils took him by surprise. This morning was just full of depressing revelations.

It was not his norm to let himself go long without visiting a barber, let alone not keep up with his stray facial hairs. But the thoughts of the incident in Milan seemed to have taken control of his daily life. Once they appeared in his mind, nothing else mattered. He shook his head and continued with his morning ritual: washed his face, brushed his teeth, and, with the help of a lot of pomade, tamed his uncommonly wild hair.

He studied his reflection again. The thought of running into someone while looking the way he did was giving him anxiety. He had to step up his normal weekend attire. Feeling like a slightly disheveled slob, Stef rummaged through his wardrobe purposefully selecting clothes that made him look or feel clean and pretty much well put together. He couldn't walk around in public looking like a commoner. Although, no one knew him in Berlin, he had a reputation to uphold. But Stef had it all figured out: rush over to the local barbershop before anyone could ever take the time to look at him. Stef liked to be looked at, and he would take his time as he passed by people, allowing them to have a good view. But this morning he needed a little fixing before he could display himself to the world. There was no way he would get back to Milan looking the way he did.

He looked up barbershops in the neighborhood but, didn't want one in the immediate area. The internet pointed him to a decent one over on Kollwitzstraße. He rushed out of his hotel, hired a taxi, and had it drive him over to the block of shops. Sure, it was a short ride from the river, but he couldn't chance being on the street.

The taxi dropped him off on Rykestrasse in Prezlauerberg, East Berlin. Stef handed the driver two extra euros without even looking at him. In fact, he avoided eye contact throughout the short ride, as if embarrassed to be seen in his current state – which he knew was not ridiculously awful, but it didn't make him feel on top.

It was a crisp Friday morning. The sunlight broke through the dissipating fog above the city, promising another gorgeous day. Friday mornings were always reserved for a light stroll to a local café. If not outdoors, he would sit by a window and watch the people pass by while he read the morning paper. This morning, however, he couldn't take his mind off of his wild hair and forest-like brows.

As Stef hurried down the sidewalk towards the barbershop, his jacket got caught on the handle of one of the bicycles parked along the sidewalk. "Damn it!" Next, he tripped over a crate of fresh fruit being delivered to the café on his left. As he straightened himself, he caught another glimpse of himself and cringed, immediately picking up his pace. He needed to be the first customer in as soon as the barbershop opened.

CHAPTER 21

THE YOUNG BARBER looked more like an ex-convict or a security guard. The sleeves of his bright white shirt were rolled up displaying bulky arms full of colorful tattoos. His smooth head and a clean shave accentuated a sharp jawline. Outside of the barbershop, the guy could appear to be someone you wouldn't want to cross. But his black apron and the dainty way he held the comb and scissors made this man an oxymoron: he could either make you handsome devil or a brutal cadaver.

With his broken German, and a lot of pointing at the photo wall of men's classic haircuts, Stef was able to communicate a simple side cut. The barber got to work massaging Stef's hair, studying his cowlicks, and combed the thick locks, separating the hair into sections. The feeling relaxed Stef. He was still annoyed he couldn't sleep in that morning. Letting himself relax in the cool chair, Stef closed his eyes and concentrated on feeling the barber's gentle fingers as they worked his head. He felt the light touch of the black comb running through his hair. His mind was letting go, finally paying attention to the soft hum of classic jazz coming from a small speaker on the wall behind them.

His relaxed state didn't last long. Thoughts of the incident in Milan and the failure of last night's burglary disturbed Stef's calm distraction on his appearance. It was supposed to be a basic routine. All the details were handed to him. He just had to do what he knew how to do best. Sure, it had been a while since he resorted to something so barbaric, but he needed the money. He kept trying to convince himself it was not a big deal. That it was just a minor set-back to this month's funding. He'd just have to wrangle another job.

"Möchten Sie sich heute rasieren?" The barber's raspy voice interrupted Stef's thoughts.

Stef looked at him through the mirror as the barber leaned down close to his face. Comb in hand, the barber motioned a shave with his ring finger. Stef noticed the flex of his bicep, confirming that this guy could definitely kick his ass, and submitted to a proper shave with a simple "Ja, Danke."

The barber leaned the chair back, forcing Stef to expose his neck. This was typically the point in the service where a man offers his trust to the one holding a sharp blade. Stef closed his eyes, succumbing to the vulnerability, as the barber gently lathered the warm shaving cream onto his face. The subtle tingling of the menthol poked at his pores, allowing Stef to relax more and more, to give in to the barber's control.

Stef felt the barber's finger steady his head, waiting for the razor blade to make contact. By nature, Stef winced at the first cool touch of the blade, and then immediately relaxed, allowing the barber to do his task. He didn't want to think about that blade running along his jaw, close to his jugular. Instead, Stef focused on the tune coming from the speaker nearby.

Since he was getting work done to enhance his good looks, his mind soon wandered again to last night's botched burglary. He didn't care much that he failed at his task. It only meant that he had to take on another job to replace that income. After all, how else could he continue to keep up with his appearance if he didn't complete an occasional little job?

He thought he'd be past the petty work by now. He was in his late thirties, spending his time with the wealthy crowd. They were all young, successful professionals who managed to make something of themselves. Stef, on the other hand, managed to find himself constantly investing in failed opportunities. But he would never let his friends know of his failures; he was too proud for that. Instead, he preferred to ignore the mishaps, continue living the high life with his peers. Stef convinced himself he was just experiencing a temporary lapse of funds. His day would come again. He just needed to sort things out. In the meantime, no one needed to know.

He opened his eyes again when the barber peeled the towel from around his neck and snapped it to the side. He then raised the back of the chair and forced Stef to lower his head, exposing the back of his neck. He proceeded to apply the warm cream along the bottom of Stef's hairline, then ran the razor with short, downward strokes. The man's fingers held his head down, and for some reason it led Stef to think of Beatrice's touch.

The shave was finally complete. The barber gently patted Stef's clean face with a woodsy aftershave. The pine-scented elixir caused a burn that lasted only seconds, followed by the soothing crispness of the clean, close shave. Stef avoided eye contact with the man when he asked for the total. For some reason he felt awkward, as if they had just engaged in some shameful act. He felt as if he was being unfaithful, but to whom? Was it Elena? Or maybe it was Beatrice. Stef shook himself out of his thoughts, paid the smiling man, and left the barbershop.

CHAPTER 22

A SMACK OF cold water to the face startled him. He drew a long, deep breath and jolted his head to the left while his eyes fluttered open to the sight of bright white and teal tiles. He realized he was sitting upright. A breeze tickling his wet face as he looked up to a man sitting across from him. The man's tortoise shell sunglasses masked his eyes. He wore a sky blue linen shirt with only the top button unfastened.

The table between them was dressed with a white cloth, white dishes, and green ornate drinking glasses. The man was just served a plate of seafood and polenta.

"Where—"

The man put up his finger and clicked to silence him. He smiled while waving to someone behind him, who immediately placed a dish of the same in front of his guest.

"You do not speak." The man's voice was coarse, deep, with a touch of elegance. "Eat your food first. Don't let it go to waste. It's a local delicacy."

"But—," As he attempted a reply, a burly hand appeared from behind him and silenced him with a forceful squeeze on his right shoulder. The guest looked again at the man across from him, who nodded to his plate, indicating that he must eat.

"I ask the questions," he said. "But first we eat."

On the plate in front of him lay three glistening, sardine-sized silver fish, accompanied by two squares of polenta. He looked up at the man again. Beyond him was a view of a blue lake surrounded by mountains.

"That is Lake Como. And what you have there is missoltini." The man spoke as he lifted one of the three small fish. "A specialty of this place. It may not be the season for it, but I managed to find some." He placed the fish back on the plate and wiped the oil from his fingers with a cloth napkin. "These little guys are fished right out of that beautiful lake."

The man proceeded to pick up the fork and knife. Gently, he broke apart the fish, allowing the oil to spread towards the polenta. He moved a piece of fish in the oil, making sure to soak up as much as possible, and lifted it into his mouth. He chewed his food with grace, looked up at his guest, and nodded with a smile.

As his guest, he felt forced to mimic his host's procedure. When the fish hit his tongue, an awakening filled his soul. The crisp taste of salt and rich olive oil heightened the clean seafood flavor of the fish – a euphoric taste of the lake in front of him.

"Do you like it?" the man asked in between bites.

He nodded as he scooped up the accompanying polenta.

"These take time to make, you know," the man continued. "They are fished in late spring, early summer. Packed in salt, hung to dry, then tightly packed in salt again with bay leaves until the beautiful autumn season, when we typically can enjoy them." The man looked at the lake again and added, "Yes, it is spring, but I find my ways."

The guest looked at his water glass, intrigued that there was no wine accompanying this man's meal. He took a moment to sip the water in front of him. It sparkled in his mouth, washing out the seafood taste and allowing the next bite to give another burst of flavor.

The plates and utensils were quietly taken away. The man took a sip of his water, then leaned back and began his interrogation.

"So, you've managed to get yourself thrown into a river. We've really selected a smart one, haven't we?" The host looked back at the lake when he spoke. "You're lucky I had my men follow you. Or you wouldn't be here, enjoying this delicious meal."

"What happened?" the guest replied, his head still throbbing in pain.

"No. You don't ask the questions. You answer mine." The man leaned in. "Where is it?"

"What?" The guest was confused. What happened to him? Last he remembered, he was being dragged from the embankment, but where to, he had no clue. As he opened his mouth to ask, he felt a sharp pain on his left hand. He screamed when he felt a cloth-covered hand cover his mouth. The pain shot up his arm, throughout his body, throbbing from hand to toe. He breathed heavily into the cloth and looked up at the man across from him.

"Where is it?" The man had removed his sunglasses, exposing a malicious gaze of patience lost.

The guest struggled to keep his head up straight. He stared into the man's eyes as the whole scene in front of him fogged over to blackness.

CHAPTER 23

Paris

STEF WIPED HIS hands with the embroidered lavender handkerchief he had taken from that Berlin apartment. He had a large collection of handkerchiefs that he had absentmindedly taken from jobs and eventually realized he was inadvertently collecting souvenirs. He couldn't place where he had snatched each handkerchief, but every time he reached for one, a memory of a job would accompany it.

He sat alone on a train, facing forward at a table scattered with crumbs left by the previous occupants. The thought of how certain people could be so slovenly and inconsiderate made him cringe. He breathed out in frustration and rolled his eyes, and that was when he had taken out the lavender handkerchief. Just as he was about to brush the crumbs aside, a train attendant came down the aisle wiping each table with a cleaning rag. When the attendant reached his table, Stef avoided eye contact by first looking at his newspaper and then down at the platform outside his window. Eventually, Stef focused on his own reflection in the glass. He was glad he decided to give up on the moustache. It was annoyingly itchy and bothered his face. Moustaches are over, he had convinced himself. He didn't need that caterpillar-like feature to augment his distinguished look. But he was lying to himself. Deep down, he really did want the moustache. He might try it again.

Stef let the attendant do his job as he watched passengers shuffle up and down the platform, or struggle pulling suitcases from a newly arrived train. The silence was broken by the soft voice of the on-board system: Ding! – "Bienvenue au TGV…," the female voice droned on with details about the route. – Ding!

The attendant welcomed him aboard and moved on to the next table. Stef adjusted in his seat, stretched and crossed his legs, and opened the morning paper.

Ding! "Si vous ne voyagez pas à Turin o Milan, veuillez débarquer. Les portes se referment en 2 minutes. – Se non si viaggia a Torino o Milano, si prega di scendere…" Ding!

Ding! "Les portes se referment. Le train partira en 1 minute…" Ding!

The train doors closed and the hum of the engines vibrated the floor beneath. New passengers were still walking up and down the aisle looking for their reserved seats. Stef was content that no other passenger had joined him. He was relieved he had the whole table to himself. That is, until a gloomy looking American walked over. Stef felt his own look of disgust; he wanted the table to himself. He wanted to hate this invasion, however he did admire the depressing man's navy blue blazer. He wanted the blazer. He had to find a way to read the brand label, to purchase one later. Although, he thought, it would be easier to just take the blazer from him.

The man put his brown leather bag on the shelf above and settled into the seat across from him. Stef smiled and adjusted himself again as he uncrossed his stretched legs to let the man into the seat. The man responded with a nod and half smile – a silent thank you with a hint of gloom. Stef hoped the man would sit quietly and fall asleep. He didn't want to engage in conversation, and especially didn't want to know why this man was so sad.

The invasion of space was the ultimate confirmation for Stef to switch seats. It bothered him more that he had to find a new seat. But, why did he have to be the one to move? He was there first. He monitored the empty seats in the car and waited for all the passengers to take their reserved spots. Of course, all the solo seats were taken. They had already been reserved when Stef booked his seat.

He folded his paper, looked up at his bag above, and planned his shuffle to another seat. He didn't want the sad man to know why he was moving. He didn't really care, but still, he didn't want to be so obvious. The train slowly departed. Stef looked up and down the aisle. Everyone was seated, sorting themselves into their spots for the long journey ahead. Empty seats were few. Aside from the other two seats at his table, there were a few available in paired seating, but always too close to another passenger. It seemed to Stef he had the best option at the moment. No one was seated next to him, and no one directly across from him. All he had was that sad man diagonally across from him, practically leaning his forehead on the window, watching the station move away. It was decided: Stef would remain in his seat and try to enjoy the ride to Turin. And maybe then, most of his fellow travelers would disembark and he'd have the car to himself for the rest of the trip. From Turin, it was a short trip into Milan, so most likely only a few people would remain. *Yes, it will be fine,* he thought to himself. *Sorted.*

He could still taste his late-morning breakfast – a croissant with a Bicicletta cocktail – that he had taken at the bar in the station's Train Bleu. The bartender had given him a judgmental look when he ordered it, but Stef didn't care. He wanted to be drunk. Besides, he hadn't slept all night, and had already had enough coffee that morning. His bag was empty of any treasure though, reminding him of his failure.

It was a stretch to try and burgle again. He knew he shouldn't have attempted it. He wasn't fully ready and he didn't have the right outfit. When he got back to his hotel room, he had shoved the black clothes into his leather bag, shaved off his shadow of a moustache, taken a warm bath, and tried to fall asleep. But he couldn't sleep. He kept thinking about the item he wanted to find in that old woman's apartment. He had studied the place thoroughly prior to that evening, and still he managed to botch the job. It was an amateur move. Maybe he shouldn't have attempted it the second time while drunk. But he was certain it was going to be an easy job. The woman was supposed to be gone for the week. Never did he expect someone to be in the place. Whomever it was had heard him and probably contacted the authorities, cutting Stef's trip very short.

He was returning to Milan, where he knew jobs would be easier for him. He knew the place like the back of his hand. And people knew him. Well, they knew him as the posh, opera-attending, cocktail-sipping, independently wealthy Stefano Orso. But none of his acquaintances knew how he really maintained his lifestyle. Whenever he was introduced to someone new, a vague description of sales or shipping passed through his lips and no one really pressed further. All that mattered was getting drunk and enjoying an elegant meal. No one needed to know how he did it.

CHAPTER 24

BEATRICE SLICED A wedge from the lime and gently placed it on the rim of the Tom Collins glass. She walked the cocktail along the bar, over to the wealthy-looking man seated at the far corner. He had asked for a simple gin and tonic, specified a top shelf gin, and flirted with her as he placed the order. He was an older man, still with a full head of hair, thick with some greys that added to his distinguished aura.

"Your gin and tonic," she proclaimed as she set the drink on the coaster in front of him.

"Thank you," he replied. He took a sip and added, "Tell me your name, sweetheart."

Here we go again, she thought, *another patron looking for more than just a drink.* Just because she worked at a bar and flirted with her customers, it didn't mean she was desperate to go home with them. She knew, however, that some men did not realize this. So over time, she got over being insulted by the come-ons and realized it was just a matter of letting them know she wasn't up for grabs. But when a man looked as handsome as the fellow sitting before her, she didn't mind flirting back.

"It's Beatrice." She placed her elbows on the bar and held her head up as she spoke. "Some people try calling me Bea. I don't let them. I don't like it because it sounds like you're just dismissing me, like meh." She shrugged her shoulders to emphasize the indifference.

"Dismiss you? I don't know how anyone could dismiss a girl like you. If you pardon me saying, you are quite beautiful. And I think you know that." The man leaned in closer as he took another sip of his drink.

Beatrice held a swizzle stick and stirred the olives in the garnish tray. She looked back at the man and noticed a familiar face peering at her from behind him, bending down slightly while winking at her. She couldn't believe he had the balls to show his face tonight *and* the courage to attempt to pickpocket the innocent man while she spoke to him. What an asshole. Who did he think he was? She decided to make it obvious to the man that she spotted someone. And she decided to call him out.

"Well, well, well." She stood up with her hands on her hips. "What brings you here?"

The man held his gin and tonic, turned to see whom she was speaking to, and was startled by the closeness of the new patron. He noticed the stranger was clean-shaven, his heavy cologne wafting soft amber, and he wore a meticulously knotted bow tie. The stranger smiled, took the seat next to him, and smiled back at Beatrice. "Whiskey, straight." When he spoke, it was as if he was putting on airs. The man wanted to punch him for some reason, but he didn't know why.

"Straight, huh?" Beatrice looked him up and down and smirked. "I thought you were into anyone or anything."

"Does that turn you on?" He said it to test out her attitude towards him. Was she angry?

"Right." She gave him a side eye and placed a rocks glass on the bar.

"And another for my friend here." He pointed to the older man. "You like whiskey, right? Two whiskeys. I'm celebrating tonight."

Beatrice added a shot glass on the bar. "You're not a straight whiskey kind of guy. We both know that, Stef." She didn't wait for his response. She dropped a couple of cubes of ice in the rocks glass, poured whiskey in it, and then poured whiskey in the shot glass. In the rocks glass she added some water and a swirl of lemon rind. She handed the shot glass to the older man. "This is for the gentleman." Next, she placed the rocks glass on the coaster in front of Stef. "And this one is for the coward." And she walked away to the patrons seated at the other end of the bar.

"Women," Stef scoffed towards the older man. "Am I right?" He held up his glass gesturing to cheer.

"You know each other?" the man scoured as Stef nodded. He picked up his shot glass, nodded, and swallowed the whiskey. "Well, thanks for the drink. Have a good night." He dropped a couple of bills on the bar, stood up, and walked away.

Beatrice and Stef were seated at a small, round table on the bar's outdoor patio along the Canal Grande. She lit up a cigarette – it wasn't allowed at the tables, but she didn't care – and held it in her fingers as she spoke.

"What the fuck are you doing here? I thought you were in Berlin."

"Well, now I'm back. And I came to see you."

"You came all this way to see me?" She looked away from him when she said it. She stared at the lights reflecting off the water.

"Yes." Stef shot down his third whiskey and slapped the glass on the table. He didn't mean for the glass to make such a loud thud, but the alcohol was loosening his control. "Well, actually I came because I kept thinking about you – about that night–" He stopped himself, and then continued, "After Berlin, I flew to Paris, thinking I would stay there for a bit – for a change of scenery." He didn't know why he was lying to her. "But I couldn't get it all out of my mind."

Beatrice didn't respond. She kept looking at the canal before them, ignoring the passersby who interrupted her gaze.

"Let's go to your place," Stef blurted out of nowhere.

"Are you serious?" Beatrice sat back and took another drag of her cigarette. She blew the smoke up towards the sky and crossed her legs. "I hadn't heard from you in days. And you think you can waltz back and I'd take you home with me?"

"Yes." Stef leaned forward. He softened his voice. "You know you want to. Let's go." He flicked his head towards the footbridge a few steps over, then added matter-of-factly, "You're done with your shift. Come on."

Beatrice squinted her eyes at him with a look of incredulity. "How do you do that?"

"Do what?"

"Just easily walk in here and expect me to take you home. What makes you think I would sleep with you?"

"Because you can't stay angry with me long. You know that." He stood up and extended his hand. She was annoyed that he was right. She couldn't resist him. She took another long hit of her cigarette and blew out the smoke with frustration.

"Come on," he repeated.

She grabbed her purse and jacket, finally took his hand, and declared, "You're not staying with me," as she followed him over the footbridge.

CHAPTER 25

STEF LAY WITH one leg wrapped under Beatrice's, who lay asleep on his left. The scent of her bedsheets was now a mix of fresh lavender and sex. He reached for her cigarette pack, slid one out, and quietly lit it up. He rested his head back down on the oversized pillow, drew a drag, and stared at the ceiling. Beatrice stirred, moaning with a yawn. She opened her right eye and then closed it as she shifted and rolled away from him, facing the window. Stef looked back at the ceiling and finished his cigarette. The morning sunlight grew stronger, exposing the small piles of clothing the two of them had thrown around the room. *What a mess*, he thought. He should go. He wanted to avoid any talk of that incident. She hadn't brought it up all evening, so maybe she too was avoiding discussing it – which was fine with him. He leaned over to the ashtray on the nightstand, put out the cigarette, and forced himself out of her soft bed.

Beatrice refused to open her eyes as the bed shifted. He was making his exit. She listened as he searched the room for his clothing and slid his legs into his pants, his belt buckle clinking as he searched some more. Finally, the clinking stopped – a signal that he was fully dressed. It was quiet. She didn't hear the door open. Was he still in the room?

"Good Morning, Beatrice." His whisper was intoxicating, but she refused to open her eyes. "Thank you for a great night," he added. She heard the door open and shut, then the faint sound of his shoes on her living room floor. Finally, the sound of the outer door closing. He was gone.

Immediately, the feeling of regret engrossed her. Fooled again. No matter how many times she told herself she was done with him, she couldn't resist his attention. With just one look, she was instantly reminded of how wonderful it could be between them. But then she remembered the bad that came along with any relationship with him, after having made a fool of herself. Once again, she lay in her recently vacated bed hating herself.

Chapter 26

THE TRAM RAN along the track up viale Romagna as Stef stared at trees on Piazza Piola ahead. He was relieved to get this meeting with Flavio over with. Berlin was another simple job that ended up being more dangerous than it should have been. After that night of running, he vowed to himself that he needed to focus on another form of income.

At Piola, Stef stepped off the tram and looked for via Fucini – a street he was sure he had never seen – and searched for the doorway he had been instructed to find. Flavio had repeated it to him three times: a yellow door with a blue lion-serpent creature painted on it.

He passed a doorway that resembled that exclusive telephone bar he had visited once. He wasn't sure if it was the place, but he gave the door the middle finger as he passed by anyway. In fact, he knew it wasn't the place; it couldn't have been. He was in the Lambrate neighborhood, which was nowhere near that fucking telephone bar. He continued down the street to via Fucini and found the yellow serpent door located in a dark corner.

The entrance to the locale was cramped. Stef had to walk down three flights of stairs to an underground oasis that resembled a bar inspired by a greenhouse. The place was very small, with only five metal tables and a metal bar that accommodated five stools.

"Well, well, Stef. You're back to getting shit done." The raspy voice appeared from behind him, crawling up his spine like a deadly insect. Stef turned around slowly with the most ridiculous smile he could muster. Flavio gestured to the empty seat in front of him, "Sit down. How was Paris?"

"Fuck you," Stef shot back as he dropped in the seat. "Paris was unnecessary. I should have just come back from Berlin. What a waste of time."

Flavio didn't respond. Instead, he slid a yellow envelope of cash to Stef and took a final sip of his whiskey.

"What's this for? The job wasn't done. You fucked me again."

"Just take it."

"Thanks." Stef picked up the envelope, looked inside, and counted the cash. "Really?"

"Yes."

"Well, I mean, I was there…"

"Just take the fucking cash and shut up."

"Fine, fine." Stef slid the envelope into his inside breast pocket. "Well, I guess now you can fuck off."

"How about a drink?" Flavio ignored him and signaled for the server.

"How about you politely fuck off?"

"Must you be so crass?" Flavio responded and then turned to the server just approaching the table. "A whiskey. And another for my friend here."

The server returned with the whiskies, and the two men sat quietly sipping their drinks.

CHAPTER 27

"BEATRICE, COULD YOU ring this check in for me? It's for table number three, in the corner," her coworker called out as she grabbed another tray of drinks. Beatrice really hated when her coworker did this. It was her responsibility to get her own checks. Beatrice was busy mixing the drinks; the last thing she needed was an order from someone else. Rather than get into another argument, she punched in the numbers and swiped the card. As the machine computed, Beatrice flipped the card over and held her breath when she saw the name.

"Beatrice, what are you talking about?" It didn't take long for Stef to respond to her text. She had frantically sent the message: *Are you close? Please come here now.* After their last interaction, it was odd for her to send a message like that to him. Maybe she wanted to talk, or maybe something was wrong. He didn't know, but was glad to hear from her.

"It's the name." Beatrice kept repeating it over her cigarette. She was sitting on the steps in the alleyway behind the bar. "Kevin Benton. It's the same name. From the wallet..."

"How is that possible? You must be mistaken." Stef didn't want it to be true. He hoped she was overreacting. "You're being paranoid."

"No, I'm not!" Beatrice threw her cigarette in a puddle, stood up, and led Stef back into the bar. "Don't you remember the name on the cards in the wallet? It was the same name. And he looks just like him, I think. Go see for yourself. Is it him? It can't be him. Is it?"

"It can't be," Stef assured her. "But, if it makes you feel better, I'll go check it out."

Beatrice cautiously took her place back behind the bar, trying not to look at table number three. The bar had quieted down even more now. She was able to concentrate on Stef's sly approach.

Stef saw the man at table three. To his surprise, it was the same dopey American who was on his train! He turned on his heels and went to the bar.

"Beatrice." He leaned on the bar, pretending to peruse the menu. "Beatrice, come closer."

"What is it? Is it him?"

"He *does* look familiar," Stef said while pointing to the menu, pretending to be asking a question about a drink. "That guy was on the same train from Paris. I remember him exactly."

"What?" Beatrice mindlessly wiped the counter. "But is it him? The man we—"

"Shhh!" Stef dropped the menu. "No, I don't think so. I don't know. But why was he on my train? Why the same train? Is he following me? Who is he?"

"What's happening?" She wanted to cry. "Stef, you have to find out."

"OK." Stef stood straight. "I'll just go there and see if I can strike up a conversation. But how? Oh, what if I deliver him a drink?"

"Deliver a random drink? No. That will look suspicious. Besides, you don't work here."

"But you do."

"No! Absolutely not."

"Come on. We have to find out who he is."

"He's getting up. He's leaving!"

"We have to find out where he's going. Come on."

"But, I'm working…"

"Go back there and put on your regular shoes, grab your coat. You're done for tonight. Pretend you're sick."

"But…"

"Hurry! He's going to leave."

Beatrice exited to the bar's back room. As she buttoned her coat, Stef slid through the door. "Beatrice, hurry. He just left and is walking around the corner. Let's go through the back here."

They waited in the dark alley for the right moment to follow the stranger. The man had taken a left outside the door and headed up away from Porta Ticinese. They followed from behind and watched him turn left towards Porta Genova.

Stef led Beatrice down a narrow street in an effort to catch up with the stranger, as he would pass directly in front of them, but as they approached him, they saw he had crossed the street.

A tram glided past them from the left, another from the right. Both trams passed each other like dancers of the night setting the evening stage for a scene to follow. When the trams separated, the stranger was gone.

"Where did he go?" Stef said aloud, looking frantically up and down the street.

"He couldn't have gotten far." Beatrice stepped out into the street, ignoring the plan to stay hidden. "He has to be close by."

Stef jogged to the right, then back towards the buildings to the left. He, too, mindlessly made it obvious he was searching for someone or something.

"He's gone, Beatrice." Stef caught up with her and took her hand. "We lost him."

Beatrice embraced him and let him hold her tight.

"Stef, what are we going to do?"

"I don't know." Stef caressed her back. "For now, we have to just hope he didn't recognize us."

"Of all places—" She dug her head into his chest. "He comes to the bar where I'm working. He must know." She dug even further into him. "Damn it, Stef. I can't believe this is happening."

"Relax, Beatrice." Stef squeezed her tight. "We'll figure this out. Who he is and what he wants. For the moment, let's just not drive ourselves into a frenzy. OK?"

Beatrice pulled away, wiped her eyes, and nodded. She rested her head on his shoulder as they walked away into the night.

CHAPTER 28

KEVIN DIDN'T KNOW where he was going or what direction; he just went underground and jumped on a train, hoping it was the correct one.

The train made another stop – Sant'Ambrogio. Kevin remembered the name. He stepped off the train and walked over to the map on the wall to get his bearings. He discovered he was headed back towards Cadorna station; however, the signs above indicated there were no more trains. He looked at his watch, it was almost 01:00. *How did it get so late?* He passed through the metal gates, which a metro worker closed behind him, and stepped up to the street. He thought maybe he would find a taxi, or figure out the tram or bus system, which he knew ran later, if not all night.

The night was quiet in the piazza. Beyond the tops of the buildings, he saw the steeple to what he later read was Sant'Ambrogio basilica. The street lights shined on the wet sidewalks. A bright orange glow beckoned from around the corner. Maybe it was a bar, where he could ask about the tram and buses or even call a taxi. Kevin walked towards the light, in the direction of the church. The light glowed from a wide shop window, workers behind the thin curtain working overnight undoubtedly creating some spectacular display inside.

He stepped through the empty piazza of the walled basilica, determined to catch a glimpse of the famous church before heading back to the hotel. He peeked through the crevice of the oversized gates at the inner courtyard, its surrounding Romanesque columns framing the famous A-frame designed basilica.

He stepped back from the locked entrance and remembered something about a Devil's column close by. The mythical column was propped up on its own to the left of the entrance. Kevin examined it for the two legendary holes that – as the guidebook had mentioned – were created by the Devil's horns, in a mythical duel between him and the patron saint of Milan.

A woman's laughter caught his attention. He turned around and saw the curtain to the shop window had been opened showcasing a furniture display. The laugh came from a slender woman with a pixie blonde haircut who stood in front of the window with a man in overalls. She pointed to another coworker standing inside the window display, instructing him to adjust the placing of a jeweled lamp.

"Bene cosi!" the woman called through the window and put her thumbs up. "Grazie!"

The man kissed her on the cheeks and walked away. The woman went back inside the shop and reappeared in the window talking to her other coworker. The man shook her hand and left the shop. Kevin heard a couple clicks of the lock, which he assumed was the woman locking herself inside.

He walked past the window when the woman reappeared, drawing the left curtain. He watched as she pulled the sheer curtain to the center. The orange light gave her face an ethereal glow. He slowed his pace and watched as she adjusted a blanket on top of the flowery divan. An oversized lavender scarf fell off her shoulder revealing her slender neck. She walked over to the ornate mirror, adjusted her scarf, and paused. Kevin realized she was looking at his reflection, into his eyes. He froze.

He couldn't really tell if she had been frightened or maybe curious. He kept staring into her eyes, hoping to give her the impression that he was not a creep. He raised his eyebrows to create an innocent look – something he had practiced in the mirror over the years. He never liked the look of his face at rest – as he got older it seemed to appear more and more like a grumpy scowl. So, he raised his eyebrows and put on a slight smile.

He knew he should probably break the stare, but he couldn't resist holding her gaze. After all, she didn't seem too concerned; she also held her stare. He watched as her eyes squinted with what appeared to be a friendly, almost welcoming smile. Was she flirting with him? Was this supposed to happen? He hoped so, but he couldn't tell.

He finally broke the connection and focused his eyes on a random object on the sofa behind her. From the corner of his eye, he saw her turn around and slowly pull the curtain from her left. He was embarrassed. He looked back at her and watched her leave with a smirk as she pulled the curtain closed, blocking them from each other's view.

CHAPTER 29

HE FELT THE softness of the satin pillow on the right side of his face. He opened his heavy eyes to an unfamiliar bedroom. He stretched his arms and yawned. The sting on his left hand reminded him of the brutal luncheon.

"Buongiorno." A man's voice startled him, causing him to reflexively jerk with surprise. The man wore semi-formal attire, like a butler from an English manor, but his accent was Italian. "Your clothes are on the chair there. Everything you need is in the water closet. Breakfast is on the table. You're leaving in an hour."

"Huh? Who are you? Where am I?"

"You'll know as soon as you come downstairs. Please don't take too long." The man kept a neutral expression, looked around the room, and closed the door.

He struggled to free his left leg that he had entangled in the sheet – which usually happened to him while in a deep sleep. He rushed to the window that was enclosed in vine-like black metal bars. He looked down at the lake and felt the crisp mountain breeze brush his face. A boat cut across to the left, reaching the dock across the lake. He watched a couple step onto the dock, then lost them as they stepped under a canopy of lush green leaves. Beyond the dock, hiding behind a wall of shrubs and violet and white flowers, was a beautiful old palace.

A faint sound of laughter floated up from below. He looked down but could not see from where the laughter had come. As his stomach grumbled, he turned to the table and lifted the cloth napkin from the plate, revealing an array of croissants and rolls with jams and butter – all of which reminded him how ravenously hungry he was.

CHAPTER 30

STEF FELT BEATRICE'S arm slide underneath his, hooking onto him as they exited the courtyard of the Castello Sforzesco. They spent the morning walking down Corso Sempione to the park, where they had just paused underneath the arch to exchange a soft yet passionate kiss. It was as if seeing that stranger at the bar last night had not happened. As Beatrice pulled away, Stef looked at her eyes, which appeared full of worry.

He didn't have to ask; he felt the same concern. Who was that man at the bar last night? Why did he have the same name as the cards in the wallet? Why did he come into that bar? Was he looking for them? Was he watching them? Did he know what they had done? There was no mention in the news of a random body floating in a river. Surely, it was not yet discovered, and would not be discovered. He hoped, in fact, that the body had sunk down to the bottom, never to be noticed by anyone. Or, if it would be discovered, there would be no ties to Milan, to the bar, to Beatrice, nor to Stef.

He had gone home to Beatrice's after closing last night. She, too, was freaking out over all the possibilities. Stef tried to engage in intimacy, hoping it would distract them, which shocked Beatrice even more. *What are you thinking?* she had asked after a hard slap to his left cheek. He had apologized, realizing what a fool he was to even go there at that moment. When they woke up that morning, she had suggested a walk to clear their heads.

They had been walking for an hour already but could not shake the vision of that man sitting at the table last night. Who was he? They kept trying to figure out the possibilities as they made their way down Corso Sempione, even stopping for another morning coffee, anything to distract from driving themselves crazy.

/ / /

Shuffled into the hall with a separate small group of four tourists – an unlikely number for viewing this masterpiece. Kevin broke away from the group, who listened attentively to the lecturer's whispered history lesson. This was his moment to have the fresco to himself. The whole scene was incredibly active. The men were all depicted in some form of realistic action, the one at the center giving a cheeky look that – depending on who was looking at it – was somewhere between inquisitiveness and sadness. Kevin swore he could even make out a smile, not unlike the Mona Lisa he had just seen in Paris. Just who was Leonardo mocking with these suspicious expressions? He stared at the face for quite some time before realizing the tour group had formed around him, staring up at the same wall, as their guide began a speech about Leonardo's technique.

Kevin stepped back to view *The Last Supper* in whole. The bright blue color of the men's robes seemed to pop the most, drawing the eye to the center of the image. In fact, most of the scene – from the angle of the walls to the actions of the men – led the eye to the man at the center. This really was a masterpiece. At that moment, Kevin was sure he had made the right decision to make this trip to Milan.

/ / /

Stef looked Beatrice in the eye, then up at the arch, and nudged her into the park. The kiss helped get their minds off the stranger for a bit, but their worry crept back. They hoped a stroll among the trees of Sempione might extend their ease – but it did not.

"Stef, do you think someone knows?"

"No." He tried to sound confident but, knew he didn't. "I mean, if someone knew, don't you think they'd approach us by now?"

"Well, I would assume that's what that man – that Kevin – was doing last night."

That was it. When Beatrice finally said it, he couldn't help himself. He stopped abruptly, dropped down to the closest bench, and put his head in his hands.

"Stef…" She sat next to him, caressing his back. "Let's try to keep it together. For each other, at least. We have each other, and that's important. Let's just keep our heads down and go on as if nothing ever happened."

"Until that guy shows up again, you mean?" He sat up, water in his eyes.

"We'll deal with that when and if he does," Beatrice replied, trying to convince herself that what she said was enough to keep them calm. It wasn't. "Come on." She took Stef's arm. "Let's go grab something to eat. Let's just enjoy something."

"Yes." Stef followed her through the Castello. "For all we know, it could be our last."

"Stop it." She hooked her arm underneath his and led them through the crowd of tourists through the courtyard, out to Piazza Cairoli.

CHAPTER 31

KEVIN HOPPED ONTO a tram and made his way to Piazza Cordusio for a quaint eatery he had read about online. The restaurant was fairly new but it was known for offering the classic specialties of the region. It was perfectly situated between Castello Sforzesco and the Duomo cathedral – both destinations on his must-see list.

He wanted his first risotto in Milan to be a good one, and according to the reviews, this was the place to go. It took him a while to find the small street behind the busy piazza, but with perseverance – mainly due to his grumbling stomach – he was not going to give up. After walking past the unassuming doorway several times, he found the restaurant merely by looking up and spotting a small hanging sign pointing to the entrance, which he had initially mistaken for a vintage shop rather than a restaurant.

Kevin opened the door to the sound of 60s music. He spotted a man sitting behind the host station, looking more like an accountant on the phone with his client. The man held up one finger to Kevin, silently signaling the question. Kevin nodded –

yes, table for one – to which the man handed him a menu that resembled a newspaper and gestured for him to wait.

Kevin didn't look at the menu; instead he took in the wonder of the vintage décor surrounding him. To his right was a set of old typewriters, each with paper rolled into the platen, and on them phrases typed in mid-sentence. Above the typewriters hung tennis rackets and framed newspaper articles, some with headlines focusing on events from the mid-sixties.

To the left was a black metal railing with stairs that led up to the main dining room that was full of talkative patrons. In the far corner of that room, he spotted hanging linens, an antique washing machine, and TV set.

"Signore," the man called out to Kevin. Next to him stood a young girl in a tight black skirt and yellow top, waiting to lead him to his table.

"Prego," she said with a sincere smile. She turned her head, letting her Rita Hayworth hair flop, as Kevin followed her up the steps.

The dining room consisted of different half levels with black metal railings. The ceilings all had laundry lines running across in every direction, from which hung table cloths and random articles of clothing. Colorful square wooden tables with mismatched seating were scattered throughout each level in a purposefully uneven spacing. Large appliances, including an old refrigerator, and a vacuum, accented the space. It was clear that the interior designer's mission was to capture the look of a 1960s courtyard in the city.

Kevin ordered a beer and perused the menu of classic Milanese specialties. He already knew he wanted the yellow saffron risotto, but he spotted something peculiar on the list of offerings.

"Scusi," he asked the server as she placed the beer on the table. "What is *riso al salto?*"

"That is risotto Milanese – you know this?" she replied. "The risotto is made *croccante*…eh, crispy!"

"Crispy?"

"Yes, it is round," She held out her hands as she said this. "Crunchy around, then inside is soft like normal risotto." She then pointed to the menu and flipped it to the English language side.

"Interesting, I will try it." He scanned the menu. "Yes, I'll have that. Thank you."

"Perfetto." She cleared the second setting of dishes and utensils and walked away.

Kevin read the newspaper-like menu with an article that described the dish. *Riso al salto* – the name literally translated to 'flipped rice'. He quickly read through the simple recipe:… *typically made with leftover risotto…knob of butter in a frying pan… add risotto and flatten with spoon…and fry until crispy, then flip…* Seemed very simple. He had never heard of this dish and was eager to experience it.

CHAPTER 32

STEF BARELY TASTED the trofie con pesto he mindlessly chewed while avoiding talking about the stranger. He couldn't stop his mind from rolling through the sketchy people in his life: the people involved in the burglaries, the ones he met on occasion during his diminishing night work, or any other suspicious person he may have encountered. Nothing seemed to connect to the guy from last night, nor the unfortunate guy in the river, for that matter. Why did that man use the same name? Was he impersonating the guy in the river? Or was it vice versa? How were the two related? Could they be the same man?

"Uff." Stef dropped his fork in frustration. "Beatrice? I can't stop thinking about it all."

"Me neither." She took his hand.

"How are the two related? Do you really think he could be the same man?"

"Stef," she caressed his hand, "I think it's inevitable. We–"

"What's inevitable?"

"We have to find out who he is? Who that man in the river was?"

"No—"

She tightened her grip. "Stef. I think we have to."

"Why?" He resisted, but knew he had no choice.

"I think it's best we get ahead of it all. If someone, or it could be more than one, who knows…"

"Oh god." Stef leaned back and rolled his eyes with worry. He hadn't even thought that there could be more than one. A group effort after them – after him.

"Let's try to figure it out. This way we can avoid what could be coming."

"What could be coming?" he replied loudly, in somewhat of a surprise. "What do you think is coming?"

"I have no idea, Stef," Beatrice whispered back, and looked around to make sure Stef hadn't caused a scene.

Stef looked around and nervously smiled at the other patrons, whom, after giving them both strange looks, had lost interest.

"Come on," Beatrice continued. "We can't talk here. Let's go get a coffee and try to figure this out."

/ / /

The server returned to Kevin's table with the riso al salto. The crispy, golden disc of rice fit perfectly in the center of the flat, white plate that reflected the lighting above, giving the disc an ethereal glow. Kevin leaned in for the aroma, then tested the crisp with a *tap, tap, tap* of his fork. He sat up, and with a final tap he broke through the crunchy exterior, allowing the steam from within to rise towards his face. The saffron and cheese aroma embraced his nostrils causing him to salivate.

He lifted his first bite and watched the steam dance seductively towards the ceiling. Gently, he blew on the morsel to cool it off before setting it onto his lips, as if to give it an inaugural kiss prior to placing it into his mouth. The rich flavors of the saffron and Parmigiano cheese caressed his tongue, giving him a jolt of excitement. It was more than he had expected, and more than anyone should ever feel over a bite of food; but as Kevin always thought, when food is good, it's *good*.

CHAPTER 33

STEF WALKED AHEAD of Beatrice, as she reached in her oversized coat pockets for a cigarette. It was the mutually understood dance of avoiding her second-hand smoke as she nervously sucked in and blew it into the air around her. She knew he hated the odor and didn't want it all over him. So, it didn't offend her that he walked ahead. She returned the lighter to her pocket and followed him through the narrow streets.

She watched as he turned the corner to the right, and followed as he turned another corner to the left. She passed a male server leaning up against a doorway of a bar, smiling at her. She looked him up and down, smiled back, and walked past as she followed Stef around the corner to the left. She took the corner and saw Stef stopped in his tracks, staring into a window across the street. She caught up to him, noticing his eyes were wide open in horror.

"What's going on?"

He put his hand up in silence and nodded to the window. She followed his eyes and gasped.

/ / /

An espresso rounded out the end of his first risotto dish. Granted, the riso al salto was a different kind of risotto dish, but it was tasty all the same. He'd have to try the classic risotto another day, so he was in no rush to leave Milan just yet.

He folded his map and returned it into his pocket. He then held the espresso cup to his face to examine the dancing figures printed around the pure white porcelain. The image reminded him of a painting he had once seen in New York. He couldn't remember exactly what the painting was, but for some reason he recalled dancing figures. The corner of his eyes caught a flicker of movement outside the window. He looked out and down to the sidewalk.

"Grazie, signore," the server recalled his attention, dropping a small plastic tray with the printed receipt.

"Thank you," he managed to reply before she walked away.

Kevin reached into his pocket, pulled out the cash, and dropped it onto the tray, with a couple more euros for a tip. He returned the rest of his money back into his pocket, causing him to lean closer to the window, where he caught the eyes of a man and a woman looking in from across the street. The unexpected connection startled him, causing his eyes to flutter. It was as if the couple was staring directly at him, but he couldn't tell. He looked away and got up from his seat. Before leaving the dining room, he snuck another quick glance out the window, but the couple was no longer there.

He got up from his seat and brushed past the patrons and the old host. He quickened his step to the exit and found no one in the street. *Why were those strangers staring at me? Who were they?* Kevin soon convinced himself it was all in his head. *No matter; they're gone.*

/ / /

"He saw us," Beatrice whispered between gasps.

"Shh!" Stef hissed as he leaned up against the building in the alley into which she had pulled him.

"Well, what were you thinking, standing there right in front of him?" she continued. "Of course he was going to see you!"

Stef ignored her comment and slowly peered around the corner. There he was, standing on the sidewalk, looking around for them. He wore a grey tweed coat; a bit too heavy for the season, but a nice tweed. The back of his head did look very similar to the man they dropped in the river. But it couldn't have been the same man. It must just be a coincidence. Maybe this was all in their head.

"He's still there." He leaned back up against the wall.

"What? Still?" Beatrice's eyes shifted left to right as she spoke.

"I'm going to go talk to him."

"Wait, what?" She grabbed his arm. "Are you crazy?"

"Well, we need to find out who he is." He gently removed her hand and continued, "Don't worry about it. I'll just ask for a lighter or something. Keep it very polite stranger-like."

He walked out onto the sidewalk and saw that the stranger had gone. He stood and looked further down the street but did not see him.

"He's gone."

"Where did he go?"

"I don't know, but he couldn't have gotten far." He held out his hand. "Come on."

CHAPTER 34

THEY CONTINUED IN the direction of the stranger, hoping to catch up with him while maintaining a safe distance. Stef kept his focus on the man's grey tweed coat and the flap of the green scarf that wrapped around his neck like a python. However, the stranger wove in and out of the crowd, with a focus on whatever mission he had set for himself. They were confident in their pursuit, until he slid into pockets of the crowd in Piazza Cordusio and disappeared from their sight.

"Do you see him?" Stef asked Beatrice while trying to peer between the people.

"Where did he go?" She pulled Stef in one direction.

"He must be headed towards the Duomo," Stef said as he pulled Beatrice forward through the crowd.

"Why would you say that?"

"Remember, while he was at the table, he was looking at a map," he continued. "I can assume that he must be visiting Milan. So…"

"The Duomo." She quickened her pace. "But, he was going north. Not in the direction of the piazza."

"Maybe he's going towards La Scala?"

"Or the Galleria?" Beatrice stopped suddenly. "Stef, he could be going anywhere."

"Well, let's stay in the area." He pulled her along. "We're bound to encounter him at some point. Let's not lose focus."

They walked to the front of the famous theatre, but there was no sight of the stranger. They crossed via Mengoni, into the small piazza. They searched the lighter crowd as they walked past the statue of Leonardo DaVinci, to the entrance of the Galleria.

"There's no way we'll find him in there." Stef looked back towards La Scala, hoping to catch sight of the stranger.

"Well, what else do you suggest? I mean, we are guessing here, Stef. Maybe he went into La Scala. Maybe he went in a totally different direction, straight to the Duomo. He could be anywhere."

"Let's not give up. We need to find out who he is."

"Stef!" She grabbed his arm. "Stef, wait a minute. Think about it."

"About what?"

"You said he had a map. While he was having lunch, he was studying a map."

"Yes?"

"And that he's probably touring the city."

"Right. Well, maybe. I mean, we don't really know."

"Stef." She looked into his eyes. "Don't you think maybe, just maybe, that he's a *no one*? Just a tourist?"

"Beatrice," Stef rolled his eyes and attempted to lead her into the entrance of the Galleria. "A *no one* that happened to have the credit cards of the man—"

"Stop it." She didn't want to hear him say it. She wanted to forget about that man in the river. She had almost convinced herself none of that ever happened. But the memory haunted her almost every night. She was relieved that he didn't finish his thought. She looked him in the eyes, and he nodded, understanding her silent gratitude for not saying it.

They held hands and faced the crowd shuffling around under the glass ceiling of the Galleria.

CHAPTER 35

KEVIN STOPPED IN the center of piazza Duomo, staring up at the massive cathedral before him. The crowd bustled all around him as he silently admired the cathedral's architecture. When he reached the steps, he was confronted by a loud tour group that had formed a long line at the entrance. Disappointed, he joined the end of the line and waited. The mist in the air had suddenly turned into droplets of rain, causing the crowd in the piazza to dissipate underneath the surrounding porticos.

The tour group scrambled to cover their heads with small umbrellas and pamphlets they had picked up along their tour. Umbrella sellers came up from underground, at almost every entrance to the Metro, advertising their convenient goods to whomever passed by. Kevin noticed the massive banners to the museums behind him. He decided to go to the closest museum, Museo del Novecento, to wait out both the rain and the tour group.

Once inside, he took his time admiring the 20th century art, including a bronze statue by Umberto Boccioni that was in the form of a figure seemingly walking through a windstorm.

Kevin climbed the escalator to the second floor – a large open space surrounded by floor-to-ceiling windows. The dark grey carpeting contrasted with the white walls that displayed minimalistic modern paintings, all of which were painted in smoky hues. The one object on the floor was a grand piano, sitting atop a short platform, overlooking Piazza del Duomo below.

Grey clouds blanketed the buildings. The rain droplets continued to strike the windows, but Kevin noticed it was now at a much softer rate than when he had entered the museum. From this level, Kevin was practically face-to-face with the façade of the massive Duomo next door. The pinkish hue of the stonework contrasted quite beautifully with the pale grey sky above. This view offered a close look at many of the sculpted forms on the cathedral: praying men, a bull, a religious figure, maybe a bishop. But Kevin was searching for something interesting he had read about in the guidebook earlier: the creature that resembled a dinosaur. There was a multitude of forms on the façade, it was impossible to search for something so specific. Maybe it was not visible from where he was standing at that moment. He wished he had read where it was placed exactly. Maybe it was something he would have to find on another visit.

The rain seemed to have subsided. Kevin looked down at the piazza, noticing the floors of the surrounding porticos were more visible and the crowd had regathered in small groups, much as it was when he stood in line earlier. He smiled when he saw the entrance to the cathedral was open and no line was in sight.

CHAPTER 36

"**THIS IS RIDICULOUS**," Stef scoffed, bumping into people shuffling through the Galleria. "It's like looking for a needle in a haystack. Let's just accept that we lost him."

"It's emptying out." Beatrice pulled him in further. "Let's just get to the piazza. If he's not there, then we give up."

"Beatrice…"

"No." She looked away and continued their trace. "We need to find out who he is. This was your idea, remember?"

"Yes, but…"

"Then let's keep going. At least check the Duomo. If he's not in there, then accept our losses." She stopped in the center of the Galleria. Around them was a group of tourists taking photographs of one another as they took their turn spinning on their heels, twirling on the testicles of the bull depicted in the mosaic tile floor.

"Beatrice?"

"Stef," She put her arm underneath his. "Do you think he'll come back to the bar?"

"As I said before, I don't know…"

"Well, I don't know why, but it just occurred to me that he would have to come back."

"Why's that?"

"Let's think about it." She urged Stef further through the Galleria. "He came in that night, clearly had a reason to. And if that reason was us, then he would have to come back."

"What about at the restaurant, just now?"

"What do you mean?"

"Well, he saw us. Standing outside the window. Do you think he knew who we were?"

"Well, based on how he looked at us…" She struggled with her response. "He did seem curious. I assume he knew who we were. He seemed interested, perplexed maybe…he looked as if he was reminded somehow. Or was that just me?"

"No. You're right. I would have to agree with you on that," Stef replied as he walked into a woman with shopping bags. "Oh! Perdonami, signora." The woman responded with a side eye and a smirk that slowly formed into a flirtatious smile.

"Come on." Beatrice pulled him away, out of the portico.

The woman could have been a potential new client, but Stef couldn't really make the connection with Beatrice there. He wanted to resist her persistence and talk to the woman, but he didn't want to expose his old habits to her. The woman was a rarity for Stef; and a reminder that these days he found it more and more difficult to land a client. But that woman's specific response was encouraging, that maybe he could still pull it off. Stef smiled at this affirmation.

"Should we go in?" Beatrice suggested.

"Huh?" Stef fell out of his thoughts. "Oh, well let's take a quick look around here before we do so."

"But with this rain, I doubt he strolled around here. I'm sure he popped into the church."

"This is not real rain." Stef put his hand out to feel the droplets. "It's a quick splutter. It's going away again. Look."

"Oh my god!" Beatrice pointed up at a palazzo in front of them. "Is that him?"

At the large window stood a man with a grey tweed coat, staring out at the piazza. They couldn't tell what he was looking at exactly, but they didn't want him to see them.

"Quick!" Stef rushed them towards the building, underneath a neighboring portico. "That's the museum's exit. We'll watch for him here. Just stay behind the plants here."

"I can't believe we found him." Beatrice leaned up against the barrier. "How the hell did we find him?"

"Luck?"

"None of this here is caused by luck, Stef," she retorted. "Well, maybe just your luck. This shit always seems to find you."

"Let's not get into this now," Stef rolled his eyes. "Focus, Beatrice. Please, let's focus."

CHAPTER 37

THE MAN IN the grey coat finally emerged. Stef and Beatrice quietly watched him look up at the sky, then up at the Duomo, and finally make his way to the oversized green brass doors. They stayed in place until they saw the man cross the front of the cathedral and enter through the entrance on the left side of the front façade.

"Let's go," Stef gestured to Beatrice.

"What? Are we just going to follow him in?"

"Of course! Let's just get this over with."

"Stef–" Beatrice didn't bother finishing her resistance. Stef was already at the steps of the cathedral. She followed him to the entrance. "Are you sure about this?"

"Mm-hmm," he nodded and dropped money onto the donation counter.

"What are we going to do?" she persisted.

"I don't know," he replied automatically in a whisper, focusing on his search for the man. "Let's take it one step at a time."

"Stef, we should have planned this better." She pulled him against the closest confessional. "We can't just walk up to him and attack him with accusations. I mean, we don't know who he is, what he's capable of, what his purpose is…"

"Beatrice, relax. We're just going to meet him."

"Meet him?"

"Yes." Stef squirmed away from the confessional. "We're going to meet him, just like normal strangers, and find out his deal."

Beatrice cocked her head and contemplated abandoning the mission.

"Just follow my lead." Stef gestured for her to follow and put out his hand.

She rolled her eyes and reluctantly accepted.

They walked to the far right side aisle and slowly made their way towards the front of the massive cathedral, searching for the stranger. Occasionally, Stef stopped them and pretended to view one of the massive round stained glass windows.

"What are you doing?" Beatrice whispered.

"Trying to look inconspicuous."

"We're going to lose him."

"Do you see him?" he said while staring at the window.

"Not yet." She slowly moved her head and looked over her left shoulder. She glanced at a small group of people admiring the main altar, but no sign of the tweed coat. "He can't be hard to find. He's got to be in here, somewhere."

"Let's keep moving." Stef prodded them to the macabre statue of Saint Bartholomew, depicted with every muscle exposed and his skin draped over his shoulder. Beatrice pretended to examine the almost-grotesque statue, while Stef stood with his back facing her, looking out at pews.

"Well?" she whispered.

"I don't see him."

"This is ridiculous." She stood straight and walked into the center aisle. Stef followed and watched her looking obvious as she searched around every column for him.

"Beatrice," he whispered.

"Shh!" She put her hand up. "He's not in here."

"What?"

"He's not in here," she replied in frustration.

"We saw him come in…"

"Wait." She grabbed his hand. "He could be up on the roof."

"You think?" Stef replied as she pulled him back to the entrance.

"Why would he go up there?" he said as he fumbled up the stairs following Beatrice.

"That's what you do as a tourist, Stef."

"No, I mean, why not see the church first? If it was me, I would check out the church, then make my way up…"

"Stef," Beatrice replied with heavy breathing. "Who the hell cares what you would do when visiting a cathedral? He was not in there. So, he's got to be up here. Now shut up and keep climbing."

"Did that sign really say 257 steps?" he replied. "We could have at least waited for the elevator."

/ / /

The clouds had opened up, allowing the sun to shine its rays on the golden statue of the Madonnina on top of the Duomo. The frame of glistening spires below her connected the rooftop, now dried and safe for walking.

Kevin stood underneath staring at the golden statuette and listened to the audio tour describe its history. The audio tour proceeded to talk about the cathedral's height. Kevin turned around, held on to a handrail while overlooking the panorama of building rooftops, and could almost make out the Alps on the horizon. The after-rain breeze played with his hair. He wondered what it would be like if he happened to slip and fall onto the crowd below. The thought of the horror and mess wiped the idea out of his mind. He declared to himself that this was not the place.

/ / /

"There he is!" Beatrice stopped Stef in his tracks. "What's he doing?"

"I suppose he's admiring the view?" Stef replied and climbed past her.

"Where are you going?"

"To meet him."

"What are you going to do?" Beatrice grabbed his jacket. "Go up to him and say, 'Hi, I'm Stef. You look like a body I dumped into…'?"

"Stop it." Stef pulled his jacket away.

"Stef," Beatrice replied.

"Beatrice, enough."

"Stef," Beatrice pulled at his jacket again. "He's looking this way."

"What?"

"Kiss me." Beatrice pulled Stef to her and kissed him deeply. He engaged.

"What are you doing?" He managed to slip out as she continued to make out with him.

"Just shut up and kiss me," she continued

Stef closed his eyes and felt her caressing his hair, his back, and his arms.

"OK, he walked away." She pushed him off.

"That was nice," he whispered and leaned in for another kiss.

"What are you doing?" She looked down at him. "Let's go." She turned to follow the stranger.

He looked down, embarrassed and followed her.

/ / /

Kevin slipped on a puddle and grabbed the handrail. He knew he shouldn't rush on the rooftop, but he had a sense that he needed to get away. Like someone was following him. The couple he spotted outside the restaurant had already given him a feeling of wariness. Seeing them again up on the roof could not have been a coincidence. They were following him. Who they were and what they wanted was not on his mind. He just felt he should flee, and that's what he did.

He descended the stairs at the pace of the people in front of him. He hoped they would step aside, allowing him a chance to quicken his steps, but no one budged. He had to hope the couple was not following him. He finally looked back up the stairwell and was relieved to not see them. When the people in front of him reached the landing, Kevin found an opening and squeezed past them, excusing himself for the annoyance.

When he reached the ground level, he quickly dropped the headset onto the counter and rushed out of the cathedral. He took a quick peek behind him, still no sign of the couple. Maybe he succeeded in losing them, whoever they were. He walked under the Galleria, crossed to the opposite end, through piazza della Scala, and turned onto the closest random street. He just wanted to get away, and at this point he felt he was far enough to stop and catch his breath. He looked back through the piazza, at the entrance of the Galleria, and there was no sign of the pair.

He walked further down via degli Omenoni, looked back towards the piazza again, and then paused to rest against the closest building. As he leaned back, he hit his head on a stone sculpture that happened to decorate the building. He stepped away, off the sidewalk, and rubbed the bump on his head. He looked back at the building and saw the sculpture he bumped into was one of six large men leaning against the stone-grey building. The men were evenly placed on the façade like decorative columns holding up the level above.

Kevin continued further down the street, away from the area, and back to his hotel.

CHAPTER 38

BEATRICE SAT SILENTLY, looking out the window of the tram. Stef had promised to meet her at her work later that evening. Should the stranger come back, he would be there to figure out who he was.

The stranger had somehow left the Duomo rooftop before she or Stef had noticed. How could they have missed him? It was that stupid kiss, she thought. It was foolish of her to go in so deep. But once her lips touched Stef's, she couldn't resist. She liked his lips. He was a good kisser, and she got lost in it. For a moment, she had forgotten all about the situation they were in. It was just her and Stef, engaging in a kiss that wasn't meant to be passionate, but somehow, naturally, it was.

And she blamed him for it. He was so good at it. Good at all of it. Immediately her mind went to all that he was good at doing. She felt foolish about allowing herself to get lost in the thoughts. Based on experience with Stef, it always led to something bad. And that kiss on the rooftop was another example: they lost track of the stranger. Not only did they lose track of him, they frightened him. He noticed them, and they scared him away.

But still, she hoped. That he did not recognize them from the bar. That he was not the same man who had "died" in the bar bathroom. And she hoped he was not the same man they had stuffed into the trunk of a car, then later dropped into a river. She hoped she would never see him again. She hoped he would just go away, that it would all go away. She hoped none of it had ever happened.

She hoped all these thoughts would come to fruition, but she knew it was all real. She knew she was stuck in all of this. And she knew she was stuck in it with Stef. She had hoped Stef and her would reconnect in some way, but never dreamed it would be over something as awful as this. Maybe this was the universe reminding her to squash the idea of being with Stef. Nothing good ever came out of it, and from the looks of things, perhaps nothing good ever would.

No matter how much he tried to ignore whoever was calling him, his phone kept ringing. He kept his eyes closed, hoping that the annoyance would stop. And when it did finally stop, he breathed a sigh of relief only to be jolted by another round of rings. He gave up on his nap. He had been sleeping for a while, he was sure of it. He reached for his phone on the nightstand and checked who was calling. It was Beatrice. He rolled his eyes, tapped to answer her call, and put the phone to his ear.

"Hello?" His voice had the crack of morning voice, after a long night's sleep, even though it was late evening. Before listening to her respond, he took a quick look at the screen and saw it was a quarter past seven. He put the phone back to his ear.

"...please? Now?" she pleaded.

"Beatrice…" He said her name slowly as he stretched out a yawn. He didn't know what she was going on about, couldn't even begin to guess what she had said, and he needed to find a way to make her repeat it without exposing the fact that he hadn't been listening.

"Stef," she continued without waiting. "You must come now."

"What?" Stef sat up and rubbed his eyes. "Where?"

"Here!" she shouted. "He just walked in. He sat at a table and ordered a drink."

"What? Who?" Stef replied automatically, then realized who she was talking about. "Wait. The stranger is back? He's there now?"

"Are you serious right now?" she retorted. "Yes! Get over here, quick. I don't know how long I will be able to keep him."

CHAPTER 39

IT WAS THE third time she dropped a mixing spoon between the stack of warm whisky glasses on the drying rack. In between each fumble, she broke two glasses, dropped a scoop of ice, and almost spilled a full bottle of vodka. Her coworkers suggested she take another break, but she didn't want to leave the area and chance losing sight of the stranger at table four.

"I'm just having one of those days," she finally replied and continued stirring a martini.

"Beatrice!" One of the dining room servers called to her from the far left of the bar. "Beatrice?"

"Huh? Oh, sure," She poured the martini into a glass, topped it with a thin lemon rind, and served it to the patron patiently waiting at the bar. "What are you missing?" she asked the waitress.

"Did you happen to take table four's order?" the waitress replied with a condescending tone. "I notice he's been sitting there for some time. I can go if you want."

Beatrice had been delaying her approach, hoping someone else would take his order, but she refused to let this particular server do the job for her. If she did, she would never hear the end of it.

"No, he's good," she replied with conviction. "He just needed some time to think it over. I'm actually on my way over there now," she added, walking away from the annoying server. She stopped at all the small tables at the bar area, pretending to check on each patron, until she approached table four.

From each table, she kept sneaking a peek at the man. He appeared to innocently peruse the cocktail menu without any hint of suspicion. As she approached, the man looked up at her, and she noticed his green eyes squinted slightly as he smiled. Immediately, the memory of that awful evening played in her mind. Was this the same man? If not, was that other man also as charming and attractive as this one? What was his story? Who was he? Who is this man? Are they the same man? She looked away, briefly breaking the polite connection between the two of them.

"Pardon," the man called out to her. His voice was deep and rough, with a slight crack. Not a voice that one would expect to come out of a man so thin and sweet-looking. She smiled back.

"Hello," she said as she approached his table, all the while wondering if he was the same man in the river. Wondering if he recognized her.

"Do you speak English?" he inquired with a look of hope.

"Yes, of course," she replied, trying not to overdo her smile. Could he see she was shaking inside? Normally, she would engage in more of a conversation, asking questions to encourage small talk. Where are you from? Is this your first time in Milan? In this situation, though, she wanted to take his order and get away from the table before he noticed that she could be the woman who had been following him that afternoon. The same woman who maybe helped throw his body into the river.

"What can I get you?" she finally blurted from her fake smile.

"Oh, great," he sounded relieved. Maybe he didn't make the connection. "May I have a Negroni, please?"

"Certo," she said and added a wink. Why did she wink? It was habit to flirt with the customers. She didn't even realize it. She was still standing at his table. She looked around, then back at him, and added, "I'll get you a water, too."

"Yes, great," he replied with a smirk. Was he looking at her suspiciously? Did he make the connection? Why had she even mentioned water? No. She had seen this look before by many other patrons before him. He was flirting with her. The idea made her genuinely smile. He smiled back and added, "Thank you…?"

"Rosaline," Beatrice replied. She didn't know why she gave the man a false name. She was nervous, so it was instinct.

"Nice to meet you, Rosaline." He stood up and offered his hand. "My name is Kevin."

"Yes, I know." The words came out of her mouth automatically. She stumbled to recover. "I mean, sorry…" She exaggerated an accent. "My English sometimes…" What was she doing?

"Oh, well, I'm sure you speak English much better than I Italian," he replied as he sat back down.

She wanted to clarify that English was her first language, but she didn't want to expose the possibility that she was deceiving him. It would only lead him to be suspicious of her and potentially connect her to all of it. She said nothing and started to walk away.

"Rosaline is a pretty name," the man said before she could get too far.

"Thank you," Beatrice replied and turned away again.

"Where is it from?" the man insisted.

Beatrice wanted to just walk away, but she wanted to keep the man in good spirits. She knew what she had to do. She would give him a story, keep him interested in her, like she used to do in her old days. Keep him involved, at least until Stef arrived. She turned around and leaned on the empty chair.

"So where did you get a name like Rosaline?" the man asked again.

"She's the girl who lived."

"The girl who lived?"

"Yes," Beatrice explained. "It's from Shakespeare. Romeo and Juliet."

"Romeo and Juliet," the man repeated, trying to remember.

"When we first meet Romeo," Beatrice continued. "He was infatuated with Rosaline, before he ever met Juliet. In fact, the only reason he agreed to accompany Mercutio to the Capulet party was for a chance to see Rosaline."

"Really?"

"Yes, and at the party, while searching for Rosaline, Romeo encountered Juliet...and well, we all know the story from there."

"Whatever happened to Rosaline?"

"Rosaline," Beatrice turned back and said. "Well, she avoided Romeo's drama. She lived." Beatrice winked at the man and walked away.

As soon as she left this table, she freaked. *What am I doing? This man could ruin me!* She felt her heart pounding, as if wanting to break through her chest and kill her.

She walked past the bar, past the toilettes, through the kitchen, and into the back office, closing the door behind her.

"Hey." His whisper came out of nowhere.

"Ahh!" She jumped at the sight of Stef tying an apron around his waist. "What are you doing? You scared the shit out of me."

"Sorry." He put his hands on her shoulders and kissed her forehead.

"Why are you back here?" she replied as she slid from his arms.

"I needed a good excuse to approach him. I thought I'd put this on, so I look like I work here, and take his order."

"What? It's already done. I talked to him."

"What?" Stef held her shoulders again. "You talked to him? Well, is it him? What did he say to you?"

"I don't know if it's him." She slid away again and opened the door. "He didn't say anything really. Fortunately, he didn't mention yesterday either. I don't think it's him. He just ordered a drink." She stepped back into the kitchen and added, "It's just odd, Stef. Why come back? It's not like he forgot what happened. Do you think he doesn't remember?"

"He didn't recognize you?" Stef ripped off the apron, put his grey sports jacket back on, and followed Beatrice. "That's great. We can go in as new acquaintances."

"What? Wait," she stopped him. "You're just going to go up to him? I don't want you to make it obvious. He may connect you to it, to me, or to yesterday."

"So, what if he does?" Stef pushed past her. "I've got this."

"Sorry for the wait." Beatrice placed Kevin's Negroni on the coaster in front of him. As the words came out of her mouth, she realized she forgot to put on the accent.

"Oh, that's OK, Rosaline." Kevin lifted the ruby red cocktail and held it up to her. "Cheers."

Beatrice smiled and watched Kevin take his first sip, relieved he hadn't commented on the missing accent. At the same time, she wondered what this man was playing at. *If he knows who I am, is he pretending not to know? Why is he playing this game? What does he want from me? Or maybe he really doesn't remember what happened to him that night. Even so, how the hell did he come back to life and find his way back here? Maybe it isn't him. Who the hell is he?* Beatrice had to get away from him before he engaged in further conversation. She turned away, leaving the opportunity open for Stef. However, she had no idea where Stef had gone.

Kevin watched *Rosaline* walk away, slide behind the bar, and punch whatever servers punch into the computer. She spun around, reached underneath the counter, and pulled out a rocks glass in which she had set a large ice cube. Her sleek black hair bobbed back and forth, brushing the left side of her shoulder and exposed collar bone.

He wanted to catch another glimpse of her eyes. He liked the way they looked at him when she spoke. They squinted slightly, giving an impression of flirting, or maybe it was just the way her eyes naturally looked. He wanted to know more about *Rosaline*. She looked somewhat familiar, almost like an actress in a classic film. And she moved with such grace; it was as if she was performing each task for an audience, yet unaware she was being watched.

His smile slowly dissipated. A sudden feeling of loss came over him. He looked away, sipped his Negroni, and allowed the sadness to take over. The sadness was clear this time. It was loneliness. Watching that woman reminded him of being alone. Sure, he had abandoned everything for this trip. He was done with it all. This was a good decision. But why was he prolonging his plans? He had decided he would do it in Paris, but events distracted him from the mission. He had forgotten all about it when he decided to come to Milan. He had never thought of Milan. Seeing the Mona Lisa sparked an unexpected interest in Leonardo, and he booked his ticket, still unsure if he was even going to use it.

Then the incident had happened, and he was distracted, and all of the thoughts, plans, mission was set aside to sort out the matter at hand. A jolt of realization had hit him. He leaned on his elbows, head in his hands, and stared down at his cocktail wondering what the hell he was doing. Why was he taking so long, and what was he waiting for?

"Pardon, sir." A strange man's voice surprised Kevin. He looked up and saw a familiar-looking man wearing a grey sports jacket. The man was smiling, and almost appeared to have a twinkle in his eye. Kevin looked down and saw that the sparkle came from a ring on his pointing finger, on the hand that was holding the empty chair to his right.

"Is this seat taken?" the man inquired.

Kevin didn't know how to refuse him without being rude. He didn't have the energy to come up with a reason to politely decline. Instead, he sat back and nodded with approval, giving the stranger the welcome to sit.

CHAPTER 40

"IT'S NOT WORKING," Stef whispered to her with frustration.

"What do you mean? Do you think he recognized you?" Beatrice replied with her hands over her mouth in shock.

"No. Well, I'm not sure, really. He's being quite elusive, it's annoying."

"My god, I can't believe this is happening. We need to end this."

"I gave him a look. I even caressed his hand again and nothing."

"What? You came on to him?" Beatrice let him go. "Are you serious right now? That's your strategy?"

"Well–" Stef looked around the corner. "Where did he go?"

"What do you mean?"

"He's not there. I think he left."

"Oh my god. Go! Go after him. Now!"

Stef jolted through the bar and out the door in pursuit of the stranger.

He stumbled off the sidewalk and onto the grooved street, wet from the rain that had apparently fallen while he was inside the bar. He looked both left and right, searching through crowds, but found no sign of Kevin nor his grey coat. He couldn't have gotten very far.

Finally, he spotted someone in a dark coat stepping underground at the Porta Genova metro stop. Stef fought his way through the crowd, dodged cars crossing through the piazza, and rushed down the steps to the underground.

Fortunately, the platform was empty, but there was no sign of the man. Stef swiped his pass and stepped through the vestibule to find only three people waiting for the next train, which, according to the sign above, was due to arrive in two minutes. A train headed in the opposite direction was pulling into the stop, when Stef looked across the platform. Just as the train pulled in, he spotted the grey coat waiting to board it.

He watched the coat step onto the train and continued to watch as the train pulled away. The coat, and the man, was lost again.

CHAPTER 41

"WHAT DO YOU want?" Stef had had enough of Flavio. He was tired of the man contacting him over and over, especially when Stef had decided he wanted nothing more to do with him.

"I want to talk about Berlin," Flavio said, and then took his first sip of whiskey and soda.

"Why?" Stef tried to hide his anger. "Why the fuck are you troubling me with this Berlin shit again? I told you: Give me another job – a different job – or leave me the fuck alone."

"No, you misunderstand. The Berlin job, it's been completed."

"What?" Stef sat up. "What are you talking about? I was there. It wasn't done. Someone else was there."

"The job is done," Flavio repeated. "We found another way."

"Ha!" Stef sat back in disbelief. "You hired someone else, didn't you? Fuck you."

"What's with the hostility?" Flavio leaned in. "You had your chance. You failed."

"And you set me up, asshole." Stef grabbed the glass and took a big swig. "Do you know how difficult it is to find work?"

"Yes, I'm sure it is. You had to learn your lesson somehow. You're not very good."

"That's not right. After all the shit I've done for you." Stef sat up and switched his tone. "What do you want? Our transactions are done. Leave me the fuck alone."

"Maybe I had another job to offer you?" Flavio sat back and looked away.

"Yeah, well, I don't want it." Stef finished his whiskey and stood up.

"Where are you going? Sit down. Relax."

Stef realized he was starting to cause a scene. He decided it was best to sit down and smile, as if there was no problem at the table. The other patrons looked away, disregarding him.

"Alright, Stef." Flavio leaned in again. "Enough of this waltz. How did you do it?"

"Do what? What the fuck are you talking about?"

"We know you're involved in this. Sure, I admit we were stupid to think he had no connection to you. He reminded us of you, in fact. That's why we gave him a chance."

"Hold on." Stef waved his hands and leaned on the table. "Just what are you saying? Are you telling me you hired someone else? Some schmuck you didn't even know? You really are an idiot, aren't you?" He sat back shaking his head.

"Don't call me an idiot. Where is he?" Flavio insisted.

"How the fuck should I know?"

"Don't play coy with me. You damn hicks all know each other."

"Woah, buddy. Who are you calling a hick?" Stef sat back up, slamming his hands on the table.

Flavio stared at Stef with a scowl, took another sip of his whiskey, and said, "I need to clean this shit up."

"I'm sure there's a broom in the back," Stef replied with a chuckle.

"Are you mocking me?" Flavio grabbed Stef's hand and gave it a hard squeeze. Stef squirmed with pain, finally freeing his hand from the tight grip.

"Calm down, man. Why the fuck are you bothering me? I have nothing to do with your fucking job. You took me out of the equation, remember?"

"You've got to help." Flavio's plea was said matter-of-factly.

"I do? That's funny." Stef propped his elbow on the back of the booth and smiled. "Why would I want to get messed up in your shit again?"

"I'll wipe your debts clean," the man said while signaling to the server for two more drinks.

"I don't owe you nothing, remember? You paid the deposit for that job."

"That's not how we see it. You're close to moving to the top of the list."

"Is that a…" Stef stopped his words when the server appeared with the drinks. Once the server had left, he continued, "Is that a fucking threat?"

"I'm just stating facts," Flavio said. He took a short sip and sat back.

"Seriously. Fuck you," Stef responded, almost shouting. He looked around to make sure no one was paying attention, then added, "All of you."

Flavio shook his head and gestured for Stef to calm down. Stef shook his head back and rose from his seat.

"Wait. Find him for us," Flavio blurted out, stopping Stef from leaving the table. "Find him and we're even."

"Find him?" Stef sat down again. "You mean...you mean, you lost him?" Stef took another sip and laughed. "Well, now, that is funny."

"Listen. Just find the guy. And find what he took from us."

"Ha! He took something from you? Wow! That is hilarious." Stef leaned in towards Flavio's face. "What did he take anyway? I mean, when you sent *me* to do the job, the item didn't seem that important."

"It was always important," Flavio replied with a hint of awkwardness. Clearly the topic was embarrassing for him.

"And you've been trying to retrieve it ever since I had tried," Stef said with satisfaction, knowing the discomfort it was causing the man across from him. Flavio didn't respond.

"It got complicated..."

"Wait," Stef insisted. "Have you been trying even before I attempted it? Just how long has this been going on?"

"That's none of your concern," Flavio replied, clearly annoyed with Stef's response. "The item has been removed. That's all that matters."

"And you can't find it. Ha! That's rich." Stef finished his whiskey and dropped the glass on the table. "Well, you deserve it. Now, fuck off."

"I'm going to let that go." Flavio stared at Stef with a stern look of disappointment. "In fact, I'm going to let you realize that you have no choice. You will help us. I'll see you soon." Flavio stood from his seat and spilled the rest of his drink on table, allowing it to run onto Stef's lap.

"What the fuck?" Stef shot up, but it was too late. The whiskey was all over his pants.

"Asshole." Flavio sneered and walked out the door.

CHAPTER 42

HE PLACED THE second glass of champagne on the brass tray, waiting for Beatrice to return from the restroom. Elena had invited him to her furniture event in one of Milan's elaborate art nouveau villas-turned-event space. He lied when he told Beatrice she was also invited, but what Beatrice didn't know wouldn't hurt her. Besides, Stef knew Elena wouldn't care.

Elena had done an impressive job placing the furniture pieces in the emptied rooms of the villa. This was going to be one of her biggest moments, hoping to catch the eye of a celebrity or other well-known names to hire her for a redesign. Her name had already been connected to powerful people, but always under the guise of the company where she had worked. Since she had ventured out on her own, she struggled to land work, even though many of the potential clients that surrounded her. They loved being around Elena and trusted her judgment on interior design. Lately, however, she had spent a lot of her time focusing on a boutique hotel in Verona. The project had taken up so much of her time that she hadn't the opportunity to showcase or pitch to potential personal clients. She didn't complain about it, though. She knew she just had to show herself and the people would come. And looking around the rooms now, the people had definitely come.

"Oh my god, I think he's here." Beatrice surprised Stef from behind. "I think I saw him in the parlor to the left. The green one."

"Are you sure?" Stef attempted to peek through the doorway, but Beatrice pulled him back.

"Don't look so obvious," she whispered. "Let's just meander around, and we'll see him. If it's him at all."

"You mean, you're not even sure?"

"Well, these days I think I see him everywhere. I don't know." She picked up a glass of champagne and sipped quickly. "What would he be doing here anyway?"

"Stef," Elena snuck up behind them. "And Beatrice, of course." She pecked them both on the cheek, allowing her lilac perfume to surround them. "Thank you for coming."

Beatrice didn't know what to expect from Elena. Last she had heard about her from Stef was that she wanted nothing to do with him. And her anger may or may not have been caused by his affiliation with Beatrice. She never addressed the issue with Elena. After all, after 'breaking it off' with Stef, Elena was not really inclusive anymore when it came to her social circle. At times, she would pop into the bar, but Beatrice was pretty sure that it probably was never Elena who chose that particular spot.

"Stef," Elena held his upper arms. "I may need you to help me with something."

"Anything, my sweet." Stef caused his biceps to flex and winked at her, satisfied with her blushing.

"Don't start with your charming shit," she retorted, removing her arms from his and then turning to Beatrice. "This guy is going to wake up someday and realize his charm won't work as much as it used to."

Beatrice looked at Stef, and together she and Elena laughed.

"Very funny, Elena," Stef waved his hands between the two.

"In all seriousness, Stef," Elena continued. "I do need your help."

"What can I do for you?"

"I have a shipment arriving at a warehouse out in Varese. The pieces are for a display later next week." Elena locked her arm underneath his as she led them both to another room. "And I was hoping you could come with me tomorrow morning. We'll get a truck."

"Are you asking me to be your date?"

"No," Elena replied a bit too quickly, and then softened her tone again. "Well, I'd just like you to be there and help me out with some things, should I need it."

"Why me?" Stef broke away gently. "Where's Paolo?"

Elena looked away, then back at him, and replied, "He won't be in town. He has a meeting in London or somewhere."

Beatrice couldn't quite understand how Elena and Stef could act as if they hadn't had an intimate relationship. Stef had complained many times about how his life was affected negatively, how he had lost many acquaintances all because he was pretty much excluded from Elena's social circle. And yet he still showed up at Elena's events, supporting her work as if she was a close friend. The two of them acted almost like a couple that had been together for a long time, or like family. Beatrice felt awkward standing in the room listening to Stef and Elena. She quietly stepped away, back into the green parlor where she thought she had seen Kevin, or the stranger who called himself Kevin. She still had no idea if it was the same man.

When Elena broke away from him, Stef felt as if he had just been swindled. Of course, he agreed to help Elena. Paolo was never there for her when she needed him. In fact, that was how Stef had first fallen into bed with Elena, filling the emotional void Paolo could never provide her. He shook his head and focused on finding Beatrice and putting an end to the idea that Kevin may be at this same party.

The adjacent room was blocked by a pack of people that had entered in that little time they conversed. Stef decided to squeeze his way through a different doorway on the opposite side of the room. This new room was much quieter; only a handful of people stood around sipping cocktails and pointing to different furniture pieces that were displayed in the space.

He looked around, but there was no sign of Beatrice. Where could she have gone? A warm hand slid underneath his elbow. The familiar scent of lilacs trickled around his nose, and he felt someone gently blowing in his ear.

"I need to show you something," Elena whispered and pulled him out of the room.

Beatrice's search for Kevin led her to the next floor up, into the bedrooms. She opened the first door to the left to a small bedroom, dark and devoid of guests. The oversized bed was covered in a puffy duvet made of emerald green satin with a sporadic scattering of etched pink flowers. She wondered if Elena had also designed these rooms.

By the window sat a marble topped vanity with brass accessories. The streetlight streamed in the window, giving all the brass a sparkling glow. Beatrice closed the door behind her and walked to the vanity admiring the marble top. The tray held an antique hairbrush, hair pins, and an empty perfume bottle. Next to the tray lay a carved wooden jewelry box. Beatrice caressed the carving of the white rose on top wondering what could be kept inside.

CHAPTER 43

HIS INSTRUCTIONS WERE simple: He was to go into the house and retrieve the item. Very similar to what he was instructed to do in Berlin. It couldn't have been easier. With the commotion of all the guests, he could hide in plain sight. After a very long drive from Lake Como, and of being continuously threatened, the message was clear: He would try anything to come out of all of this alive. He had no choice. He had to do their bidding. After all, he was fortunate to still be alive after failing them in Berlin, in Paris, and Milan. So, really, part of the job he had been hired to do was completed. There was just one small mistake that had put him in the situation he was in now.

He walked into the villa without stopping to give a name to the two in charge of checking lists. He immediately grabbed a glass of champagne, slowed his pace, and smiled at people, intending to give the impression that he belonged and had been there for a while. Pop music blared through speakers scattered in various rooms. He knew what he was looking for and entered every room, examined each piece, looking for it, all the while continuing the façade that he belonged.

He turned to the right and looked in the doorway to the next room, where he noticed a woman quizzically staring at him. Her dark hair flat with wisps of cowlicks dancing around her ears. She was beautiful. Had it been any other circumstance, he would have approached her. He noticed her glare. Did they know each other? Or maybe she had caught on that he didn't belong. She started to walk towards him when he broke his gaze and wove through the crowd in the opposite direction.

The woman had looked familiar to him, but he couldn't quite place where he may have seen her. He snuck up the stairway to the second floor and slid into the first empty room he could find. He turned off the lights and sat in the darkness. He decided to lay low, hoping the woman would give up her search for him.

The door opened. He hid behind one of the heavy green drapes hanging by the window. He watched a woman step in and admire the semi-dark room. She gently closed the door behind her and didn't bother to turn on the light. *Does she not belong here either?* he wondered, continuing to watch in silence as she walked to the vanity by his window. The streetlight lit up her face, revealing that it was the same woman that had been following him downstairs. *Who is she? And what is she doing in this room, in the dark?* He watched as she caressed the marble vanity top. But it was when he saw her caress the carving of the white flower on the wooden jewelry box that he surmised she may be after the same object. *Who is she?*

CHAPTER 44

BEATRICE LOOKED UP at her reflection and followed the light from the streetlamp glow on the left side of her face. The dim lighting was a veil on her age, which had started to show around her eyes. She had tried new techniques in applying cover-up, different eyeshadow applications, and any other new suggestions the make-up clerks provided to her to little effect.

The flatness of the right side of her hair had formed a slight wave. The humidity must have thickened to make her carefully plated hair curl. She picked up the brush laying on the vanity and ran it through, but it only created more volume. To even it out, she brushed the other side, giving up on the flat look. The waves became more prominent, and curled onto her face. Looking around for something to tie up her hair or clip it aside, she opened the etched wooden box that sat by the assorted perfume bottles. Inside it contained a silk scarf wrapped around a folded piece of heavy paper, possibly a note. She reached for it and felt something had been wrapped inside of it. She held the scarf in her hand as she carefully unfolded the paper, revealing a bronze bracelet with intricate etchings of flowers, similar to the white one on the top of the wooden box. The bracelet appeared to have been handmade. She held it to her wrist and admired its detail glistening in the ray of light. To have been carefully wrapped, it must have some value. She knew she shouldn't go through Elena's things, but it looked really beautiful on her wrist. She clasped the bracelet and admired it again.

A woman's laughter was heard on the other side of the door. Beatrice stood still, careful not to make any noise. She heard a man call out to the woman, both passing the door and continuing down the hallway. Beatrice carefully got up from the chair and stepped over to the door, listening to make sure they had left. Instead, she heard them talking.

"Oh, how I've missed you," the woman let out in a long deep breath. Then silence.

"Well," the man replied in increments. "I'm…here…now…"

Silence again. The voices sounded familiar. Beatrice was convinced it sounded like Stef. If it was Stef, who was he…

"Elena," said the man. "Elena…"

"Quiet!" Elena's voice was soft but sharp. "Get out of here. I can't believe I'm falling for this again."

"But, I thought…"

"Oh, I know what you thought, Stef." Elena appeared to have moved back down the hallway. "I refuse to fall into your traps, Stef. It's probably best you leave."

"But, I still want you." Stef followed her. "You can't just shut me out like that. Not again."

"Aren't you here with someone else?" Elena's tone was anger, with some sort of power to be able to throw that jab at him.

"That's not fair. She's only…"

Silence again. Beatrice put her ear to the door, hoping to hear more. She heard heavy breathing. They had returned to her door. In anger, she wanted to burst open the door and catch them at it. But in fear, she could barely move. She didn't want to get caught listening in on their private moment, nor get caught in a room which she probably shouldn't have entered.

She reached down to the doorknob, and when she heard the pair breathing heavier, she clicked the lock closed, preventing the chance they may try to continue their tryst in this particular bedroom. Immediately after she had clicked the lock, the doorknob was jostled from the other side.

"This one's locked," Stef said in between breaths.

"What?" Elena replied with heavy breath. "Come on."

The pair seemed to have walked away, behind another door further down the hall.

Beatrice walked back, bumped into the bed behind her, and sat down with a tear in her eye. She didn't want to feel this way but couldn't help the emotion that overcame her. She still desired the jerk. And the idea of him being with Elena again hurt her. He clearly had no dedication, no shame, nor the ability to control his urges. He didn't care.

She put her head in her hands, feeling like a fool. She knew he wouldn't change his ways. At that moment, she realized she wasn't going to be able to make him be someone he was not. If he did have any sense of feeling for her, or any idea of wanting to be with her, he would not be doing what he was doing with Elena right now. The prick.

She composed herself, walked back to the door, and listened for any signs of someone on the other side. Silence.

/ / /

He quietly slipped out from the curtain, watching the woman listening at the door. Preoccupied with whatever she had been hearing, he would be able to take the box and slip out onto the balcony. The box sat on the vanity, opened but empty. She had taken the contents. He thought he could sneak up behind her and take the bracelet from her. He carefully stepped towards her. He stopped himself. *Surely,* he thought, *she'll scream.* He had to be careful. How would he prevent her from screaming? Cover her mouth, but that would only temporarily quiet her. Knock her out somehow? He looked around for some type of heavy object. A large vase sat on the table behind him. *It seems cartoonish, but maybe it can work,* he had convinced himself. He looked back at the woman, her hand now on the doorknob.

/ / /

Beatrice had carefully turned the knob, opened the door ajar, and peeked out to confirm there was no one. The coast was clear. She stepped out quickly and carefully closed the door behind her.

She rushed down the stairs, through the party, and into the sitting room, searching for her coat by the green divan by the window. It was then she noticed she still had the scarf in her hand and the bracelet around her wrist. *Shit! These belong to Elena. Well, fuck her,* she thought. *If the sophisticated woman was taking her opportunity with Stef, then surely I shouldn't feel an ounce of guilt taking these from her.* She found her coat in the pile, stuffed the scarf in the large pocket, and rushed out into the night.

/ / /

He was about to swing when she opened the door unaware and slipped out, closing the door behind her. *Shit!* He couldn't lose her. She had the piece. He reached for the doorknob but heard people on the other side. *Shit!* He ran to the window and looked out over the balcony, which overlooked the main street below. Clearly, he couldn't attempt to crawl out. He looked for the car that had taken him there. The two men were both leaning on the car arguing, one waving away the smoke coming from the other's cigarette. He scanned onto the street and watched for her. He had to get out of the room. Or maybe he could grab their attention. They would help.

He picked up the brush from the vanity behind him and threw it at the men. The brush flew past them into the bushes. They looked around, like two idiots looking for a mystery critter. He grabbed a compact mirror and flung it toward them. The mirror hit one of them on the shoulder, causing the man to look up and spot him on the balcony.

He pointed to his eyes and then down to the front door, hoping the men would understand to keep their eye out for someone. At that very moment, the woman walked out of the door. He pointed to her, hoping the men understood they needed to stop her. She walked to the right down the street. The men looked up again, seeing his signal to keep quiet and follow her. One of the men nodded and walked into the fog, in the same direction of the woman. The other entered the house, hopefully, he thought, to help him out of the room.

CHAPTER 45

BEATRICE SAT AT the tram stop and wiped her now curlier waves away from her face. She blew one annoying lock from her right eye. The humidity had created a thick fog on the street. She reached in her pocket and pulled out the newly acquired scarf. She used it to tie her hair in a bunch, keeping the even more voluminous curls up away from her face. She almost forgot the bronze bracelet on her wrist. She caressed it with a sense of pride in lifting her new accessories from that pretty bitch.

She couldn't get the picture out of her head. Stef and Elena doing lord knows what in a dark room, as if she hadn't even existed or didn't matter. Did either of them care about anyone else? They hated each other but couldn't seem to keep their hands off each other. As if their attraction erased everything else around them. Beatrice was very familiar with that feeling. Anytime she had engaged with Stef, she immediately felt some sort of shame or guilt. Not for what they had done – because surely, it had been good, as always. The shame was for falling for him all over again, for the inability to resist him.

She looked at her watch, then along the tracks, hoping for a sight of the tram's bright lights cutting through the now even thicker fog. No lights in sight. The tram clearly was not close. If only she had left before the metro lines closed for the night. She was fumbling in her pockets for a cigarette when she heard footsteps to her left. Through the mist, she could see the figure of a man, instantly causing her to tense up.

Strange how the sight of a strange man can do that to a woman. An unfortunate price of being a woman. She had always been told to be aware of strange men, especially when she was alone. She refused to fear all men, refused to believe they were all dangerous. She refused to allow herself to think the worst without any indication of peril. However, she had learned over the years that men could truly be evil.

Growing up, as she grew into her body, she noticed how boys looked at her differently than they had before. Not only the boys, but the men around her. Whether it was a teacher, a coach, a store clerk, a bus driver, or a fruit vendor; they all looked at her differently.

She remembered the moment she first feared the opposite sex. She was fourteen, at a party at a friend's house. Everyone was talking around the table in the back courtyard. The boy she liked was sitting at the other end of the table flirting with what was probably going to be his girlfriend. Beatrice had left the table to help her friend in the kitchen. She began washing the dishes when the boy entered the kitchen with a pile of plates. Her friend took a platter out of the refrigerator and brought it out to the guests, leaving Beatrice alone at the sink with the boy standing beside her.

"May I help you?" he said as he picked up a wet platter and dried it with a rag.

"Thank you," she replied, barely looking at him through her side eye. "You don't have to. I just thought I'd help..."

"I thought I'd help too," he interrupted her. "Besides, I needed a little break."

She fumbled with the glass she had been rinsing, practically dropping it into the sink. She felt her face flush with heat. She was sure she was red. Her eyes shifted left to right with a nervous reaction. She tried to remain calm. Her heart was beating faster. Was it loud? She tried playing cool, as if the boy next to her meant nothing.

"You seem nervous," he blurted.

"What?" Clearly she couldn't hide it. She looked over at his smirk. "Oh, I almost broke this glass. I hate the sound of breaking glass. It just makes me nervous."

"Well, we all have our quirks, don't we," he chuckled and put the rag down. "Say, want to join me for a cigarette? Come on."

She followed him to the balcony that overlooked the main street. They sat on the swing and shared a puff of the one cigarette he had pulled out of his pack.

"You sure you don't want your own?" he said in between puffs.

"Yes, I'm sure." She wiped the hair from her face. "Truth be told, I'm trying to stop. I've been doing good for a while too."

"Oh! I'm sorry. I didn't mean to tempt you." His smile was different. He was flirting.

"No, no temptation here." She played it cool. "I have one now and then. Slow and steady, I will stop altogether."

She barely finished the sentence when his lips smashed into hers. Shocked, she leaned back, away from his face, but it only made her susceptible to his advancing on top of her. She struggled to push him off, but he insisted. She pulled her mouth away from his.

"What are you doing?"

"Come on." His grasp tightened. "No one will see us here."

"Stop it!" She slapped his right arm with one hand, while pushing his chest away with the other. "Get off of me."

His hands were all over her. He managed to slip one up her shirt, cupping her breast over the bra, and continued his attempts to kiss her.

"Stop!" She pulled his hand out of her shirt and kneed him in the groin.

"Ow!" he yelped and keeled over. "What is wrong with you?"

She jumped off the settee, adjusted her shirt, and stormed back into the house. He grabbed her arm and pulled her back onto the balcony.

"What are you doing?"

"Don't say anything," he whispered in her ear. "Keep this to yourself."

"What?"

"You say anything, I'll make your life hell."

"Over this?" she replied with sarcasm.

"Yes, over this." He pulled her into the house, down the hall, and into a room. He locked the door and flung her onto the bed.

"What are you doing?" She rolled off the bed toward the opposite side of the room.

"Just relax." He stepped closer to her. "Let's just enjoy the moment."

"Open that door," she demanded. Well, she tried to sound demanding. To this day, she still doesn't know if she did.

"Relax." He sat on the bed. "Just sit down. I want to talk to you."

"You sure have a funny way of asking a girl to talk," she replied. She had to find a way out of the room. Maybe making him put his guard down would help. That was when she smiled, a gesture she regretted to this day. That damn smile changed her fate in that room. It was the moment the boy assured himself what he was about to attempt was OK.

He stood up, grabbed her by the arms, and pinned her onto the bed. He threw himself on top of her and attempted to kiss her while adjusting his position, forcing his pelvis onto hers. He maneuvered on her with force. She tried wriggling out from under him, but it only made him enjoy it more. She refused to let him get his lips onto hers.

"Stop!" she yelled. "Get off of me!"

"Shhh…," he whispered. "No one can hear us."

She tried to roll them both off the bed, but he was so strong. And every move she tried to make only made him enjoy it more. She remembered feeling trapped and powerless. He was doing whatever he wanted and she had no choice. Her attempts to escape failed her. It was the moment she had stopped resisting. It was useless. She remembered thinking that he would eventually stop. That maybe her fighting him was making him enjoy it more. That maybe he was just into the chase, the fight. But he didn't stop. He continued his attempts to kiss her, continued his writhing on top of her. And she had no choice but to let him do whatever he wanted. She hoped it would be over fast, but then came the heavy knocks on the door.

The doorknob turned and swung open. Another boy came in, grabbed the boy on top of her, and punched him. She thanked that boy, but his response was full of anger.

"Get out of here," he snapped at her. "Just go home."

She flung herself off the bed, ran through the hall, found her coat, and rushed out the door. She remembered crying the whole way home. She remembered wiping her face as she neared her house, trying to hide any evidence of her wails. She didn't want her parents to ask questions. In fact, she didn't want to see anyone. She wanted to sneak into the house and up to her room with no interactions. Fortunately, she was able to do so. She undressed, got into the shower, and sobbed with shame.

She remembered laying in her bed, realizing that her mother was right, that boys are dangerous. She didn't want her mother to be right. She focused on the boy that rescued her. He saved her. He was angry about it, which confused her. But he rescued her. There are good ones out there, she knew it. Eventually, she did tell her mother what had happened, focusing on the boy that rescued her. And all her mother had to say in reply was, "You still never know which ones are the good ones."

It was that moment that influenced her to take self-defense lessons. If she ever found herself in a similar situation, she would know how to handle herself. Unfortunately, she had to use her newly acquired skills many times after that.

The fog continued to fill the street, making it difficult to see any approaching vehicle. Beatrice was still seated on the bench and noticed that the man seemed to be approaching the tram stop. Although there was no indication of him doing so, she was not in the mood for his advances. She casually stood up and continued down the road towards the Duomo – she was sure to find a late night bus or tram running in that area.

Her pace was slowed by the thick cloud of fog that had now settled onto the streets. It was difficult to follow the sidewalk, but the thick beams from the streetlights helped guide her. Lights passed across the end of the street in front of her, belonging to a small garbage truck that continued its late night rounds.

Beatrice was startled by laughter from a couple that appeared in front of her from out of nowhere. Anyone could emerge from within the thickness. Her body tensed again with the idea of some strange man, or group of thugs, popping out to take advantage of the obstructed visibility. Yes, anything could happen at that moment. It would be very difficult to pursue the culprit, let alone notice that there was anything going on, or that there even had been a victim.

She quickened her pace. She just needed to get herself to the open piazza, where visibility was sure to be better. Footsteps behind her grew louder. She looked back but saw nothing except for the glow of a streetlamp a block away. As she turned her head forward, she thought she saw something or someone appear in the beam of light. It was the silhouette of a man. He stopped, turned, and headed towards her. She jumped into the shadows and stood still on a stoop hoping he had not seen her. The footsteps stopped. Was he still there? She couldn't tell. She looked to her right and could see several glowing orbs floating in the air. It was the lights in the piazza. She was close. She stepped off the stoop and quickened her pace towards the piazza. She stumbled off the sidewalk, almost falling into the street. She caught a garbage can and steadied herself. That was when she heard the footsteps behind her again. She screamed as she felt the strong grip on her arm.

Chapter 46

BEATRICE CONTINUED TO scream until she was able to shake the hand off her. She ran towards what would be the Galleria. She needed to put herself in a well-lit area. Unfortunately, at that time of night, the area was only softly lit.

She ran down the sidewalk of what must have been a main street, but she knew it wasn't at the piazza. She saw bright lights and continued towards them, not looking back. She heard the footsteps behind her. Whoever it was that grabbed her was following her. It looked like La Scala theater was the goal ahead. She skipped off the sidewalk and crossed the street, hoping the person following her hadn't seen her. The fog was so thick that in unlit spots she could remain hidden just five feet in front of someone.

She made it to the glowing lights, which shone from inside the large display windows of a bank on the corner. The footsteps behind her had stopped. She stood in the beams of light like an open target for whatever was to come next.

"Posso aiutarla, signora?" The man's voice shocked her whole body. She couldn't tell from which direction it had come.

"Yes," she replied. "I'm being followed."

The footsteps quickened; it was her pursuer that had called out to her. She jumped out of the foggy beam and ran down a dark street to her right. Midway down the street, she stopped. She didn't want him to hear her footsteps. She looked back and saw his silhouette again. This time the silhouette was more clear. She noticed he had a long coat. And in his left hand was what looked like a gun.

With this sight, she took in a deep breath, leaned against the building, and tried her best to remain quiet. He took one step off the sidewalk, as if continuing down the main street. He stopped in the middle of the street, listening for any sound of her. She watched him silently. He looked down the dark street she was on, then looked back towards the theater.

She needed to find an open space where he wouldn't be able to approach her. Or she needed to find a place to hide. The man continued towards La Scala, leaving the area. Beatrice breathed out in relief. She quietly continued down the street and crossed the soft light from what appeared to be an opening to the Galleria. With relief, she stepped inside the lit area, where there were sure to be other people. As she passed one shop, she spotted the man. He had probably entered from piazza della Scala. He noticed her and walked towards her. She turned around, ran back to the street, and turned left, hoping to reach piazza Duomo.

She needed someplace to hide. She pressed the button for a glass elevator that would have led below ground, but decided it may not be the right choice. She backed up to a large door behind her. As she leaned up against it, the door pushed open causing her to fall over. She heard the man's steps grow faster and louder. He must have heard her and was getting close. She ran down a corridor into a courtyard. The doors were all closed. She tried a couple, but they were locked. An elevator. She pressed the button, and the doors opened. As she stepped in, she felt a brunt force push her to the back wall of the lift.

The man was against her; he had pinned her to the wall. The elevator doors closed and lifted towards the top. She struggled to fight the man off. His arm reached around her, pinning her arms to her. She was constrained. She felt his other hand yanking at her hair. She wiggled her way out of his grasp. He knocked her to the floor. She was on her knees as he bent over her, yanking her hair. Maybe it was the pain and the fear together, she didn't know what possessed her. With her left hand, she made a fist and swung it straight into the man's crotch. He moaned, bent over. As the doors opened, Beatrice rolled out onto the floor.

The cold air brushed all over her. She was on a rooftop. She picked herself up, catching her breath, when she heard his steps on the metal grate. He was still after her. She grabbed the railing and ran up a set of steps, along a walkway with the glass ceiling of the Galleria to her right.

The walkway stopped to a view of the Duomo. The beams of light glowed on the gold Madonnina statue at its peak. Beatrice looked down and saw that the fog had started to dissipate in the piazza below. She heard his footsteps, slow, one at a time. He was close, but she knew he couldn't yet see her.

"You're trapped," the man's voice was coarse.

Beatrice refused to speak. He clearly was trying to find her from her voice or any sound she would make. She had an idea.

"Who are you?" she asked as she moved to the right.

The man did not respond, but made a clunk when he slammed into the railing.

"Where are you?" he grunted.

She saw his silhouette right in front of her. She had to be quick. She ran to him and pushed.

"Woah!" The man easily lost his balance and fell over the railing.

Beatrice breathed in shock. She carefully stepped to the railing and saw the man hanging above the glass ceiling of the Galleria. He looked up at her with worried eyes. She stared into his eyes in silent shock. She watched as he attempted to pull himself up, but struggled to keep his grip on the slippery bar.

He stopped moving and looked up at Beatrice again. She saw his eyes change from struggle to defeat. He tried to strengthen his grip again but failed, and he crashed through the Galleria's glass ceiling below.

Beatrice froze in shock. She hadn't expected that to happen. She leaned in further, looked down through the broken glass, and saw the man's still body. Dead.

She ran back down the metal path and found a door to a stairwell, which took her to the piazza Duomo. Without a second thought, she ran across the piazza, away from the scene, away from the sirens blaring into the night.

CHAPTER 47

HIS LEFT CHEEK stung from the fourth or fifth punch. His ribs throbbed from the kicks. His lungs wheezed to recover from the left and right hooks that rammed his stomach. He lay on the ground, his right cheek on the pavement, staring out at the lake while three pairs of black shoes circled him, each taking a turn with a kick to his back, his shoulder, or his legs.

He had tried to fight them off, but failed in his attempts to wriggle out of the arms of the one that was holding him. They had thrown him in the trunk of the car and driven back to the house on the lake. The burly one forcefully pulled him out of the trunk, never letting go of the tight grip on his forearms. He dragged him to the terrace at the back of the house, where the punches began.

In between blows, they reminded him of their disappointment. He had failed again in getting what they wanted, and as they had claimed, they were just following orders. One of them spit in his face, while another punched him in the ribs. He couldn't muster standing anymore. The man holding him gave up his grip, throwing him to the ground, which is when the kicking began.

He lay there, silent. Both the kicks and the insults softened. He closed his eyes, hoping the nightmare would soon end. He heard one man walk away, followed by the sound of a lighter sparking and the long drag on a cigarette. A second man shouted over to someone further out – probably the first man that had walked away – and seemed to have followed him.

He heard the soft pace of one man. He opened his eyes and saw that it was, in fact, only one of the men left with him. The man was leaning on the banister, smoking his cigarette and looking at the lake. He watched the man flick ashes over the railing as he stared out to the first indication of sunrise on the horizon.

He continued to watch the man as he quietly propped himself onto his knees. He struggled to breathe but focused on remaining silent. This was the first time he felt he could potentially get away. He looked around the terrace for something he could use to protect himself. To his right was the white metal dining set. He thought if he could pick up the chair, he would swing it at the man, knocking him over the railing. But the noise could call attention to him. He looked around the terrace and saw no sign of the other men.

He put one foot down on the ground and flinched. The movement was painful but steady. He could do it. He would pick up the chair. He lifted himself up to standing, trying not to groan from the pain. The man still had not noticed anything happening behind him. He was now focused down at the phone in his other hand, probably sending a text or something.

The metal chair was cold under his grip. He had to be quick. He grasped the chair by its back, lifted it, and quickly swung it, knocking the man to the ground. The man did not make a sound.

He watched as the man slowly roll, trying to steady himself, so he quickly lifted the chair again and knocked the man out cold.

The chair hit the ground, causing a loud bang. He had to run. He looked over the railing for some type of escape. Three small boats sat tied at the house dock. He rushed down the stairs to the dock, untied all the boats, jumped in one, and with all his strength, he painfully rowed as far as he could into the lake. The other two boats drifted in each direction, leaving no way for anyone to follow him.

He couldn't row too long. The pain was dreadful. He rested his arms on his thighs, lowered his head, and watched blood dripping onto the floor. Rubbing his forehead, he felt the culprit – a gash on his left eyebrow. He reached in the water and washed his face. He wanted to sleep. He looked back at the house and saw no sign of anyone on the terrace. Maybe they hadn't yet noticed their crony on the ground and their prisoner missing.

He lowered himself further into the boat, rested his head on his hands, and closed his eyes. The boat continued to drift further into the lake, under the rising sun.

Chapter 48

THE WAREHOUSE WAS located in the outskirts of the city. It took about forty minutes to get there from Brera, where Elena's interior design studio was located. Stef had promised to help her deliver a new piece to her exclusive client. He thought it would be an awkward forty minutes, but Elena seemed to always act as if life was fine. It was as if nothing ever happened between the two of them. Did she just disregard him? Did he mean nothing to her? Her inability to show her emotion always hurt him, and every time he saw her smile, laugh, joke, or giggle, it was a stab to his ego. He just wished she would let him know she was hurt. He convinced himself that Elena felt hurt by him but was very good at hiding it.

He wanted to hate her but couldn't. They had some unexplained bond, and whatever she wanted, he never gave a second thought to being available to her. When Elena had asked Stef to join her with this particular delivery, he did hesitate a bit, but in the end acquiesced. And no matter how Elena felt about him, Stef was a guaranteed charmer, and he knew being by her side helped a lot with her most upscale clients.

"Oh, that is lovely," Elena broke the silence.

"What's that?"

"Well, apparently, we are invited to lunch at this client's villa," she explained and looked up from her phone. "He has this gorgeous villa on Lake Como; it's just beautiful."

"Well, you obviously can't turn that down."

"You don't mind, do you?"

"Mind?"

"Well, we will deliver the pieces and stay for the luncheon."

"But, am I dressed for a luncheon?"

"Oh, yes, it's casual. You have your sports jacket, you're fine. Besides, it's not like we will be moving the actual pieces. We're just driving them there." She petted his shoulder. "You won't get a spot of dirt on you."

Stef smirked at her. He felt his cheeks flush. He wanted her right there, at that moment. He enjoyed being around her. He liked the small intimate exchanges like the one they just had. Elena looked back at the road and directed him onto a small street.

"You can park over there, in area B," Elena instructed him as he pulled through the gate. She stepped out of the vehicle and continued with her instructions. "Please back up in dock 4B. I will meet you at the dock."

"Of course," Stef replied with a smile. He didn't want to show the pain she was inflicting on him.

Chapter 49

HE AWOKE WITH a jostle and a sudden intake of breath. The morning sun pierced his eyes, forcing him to flinch. He struggled to sit up. The boat continued to jostle. He looked out over the water and saw the morning activity had commenced. Small boats coasting by, a large ferry in the distance. No sign of the men. Did they not bother to look for him? Had he truly succeeded in his escape? He had no idea from what direction he had come. He needed to get himself to shore and find a way out of the area. His head pounded; he probably needed some medical assistance, but brushed it off as thirst and hunger.

He turned on the motor and steered his way toward the coast. He had never driven a boat nor had any idea of the rules or laws for boating. He kept his path straight, slow and steady, avoiding any incidents with passing boats. The engine putted and died, but the boat continued on its path. He tried turning the engine, but it struggled to reanimate. On his fourth try, the engine revived and he continued towards what appeared to be some cave-like doorway. As he got closer, he saw boats inside. They seemed to have been tied to a covered dock. He didn't know how to stop his boat, so he turned off the engine and let it drift. As he got closer, he jumped into the water and swam to the dock. The boat continued to drift further down the coast.

The holding was square in shape and had two boats tied to a tiny wooden dock, with stairs that reached up to a door. He climbed up the stairs to the door, but it would not open. It was locked from the other side. Through the opening, he saw mediocre grounds with a path that led to a small house. He hoped that whomever was in that house would need to get to his or her boats that morning. He needed to think of a way to sneak out without being seen. The door was old, probably an original, made of thick wood and iron accents. He put his face to the opening again, and to the left he could barely see a basic lock hanging in a loop. He jostled the door and saw the lock bouncing with ease.

He ran back down the stairs, looking for some other way out. Other than out into the water, he had no way of leaving the area. Unless he wanted to swim again, he had no choice but to wait. He thought it was probably best to hide for the moment. He climbed into one of the boats and covered himself with a tarp. His head was spinning again. He had to eat something. He needed to distract himself from the pain. His eyes were heavy. He eventually closed them.

"Not a problem, Lieutenant," a woman's voice said among the jostling of keys and kicks at the door. "It's a bit of a project to get this door open. We've been meaning to get it fixed."

He had just stepped out of the boat when he heard the commotion. He didn't know what to do. He snuck into the dark corner of the dock as the sound of the door up the stairs squeaked open.

"I apologize for the resistance earlier," the woman continued. "It's just that we hadn't heard of any criminal on the run in the area."

"This will be quick," the man replied in an all too familiar voice. Was it one of the men that kicked him last night? He couldn't see.

"Please go on," the woman urged him. "As you can see, it's just two boats. Nothing more."

He was now leaning up against the wall, underneath the stairs. He watched as they slowly descended.

"You don't have to come down with me," the man said back to the woman. "He could be down here. It could be dangerous."

"Well, I've got you here with me. I'm OK."

They continued to the bottom and stopped.

"That tarp was moved," the woman breathed in. "My goodness, was he here? Is he here?"

"Shh!" The man pushed her aside. "He could still be here."

"Excuse me," she scoffed. "Is that how you treat a lady?"

"Shut the fuck up, you damn bitch!"

"What?! I shall report you—"

"Report me to who, exactly?" The man pushed her aside and looked in the boat.

"I cannot believe you!" The woman grabbed his arm. "You need to go immediately. I want you off my property, now."

"Just a second," the man brushed her off.

"You're not the police, are you? Who are you?"

"None of your fucking business." He grabbed both of her arms. "Now, be a nice lady and shut the fuck up while I do my job."

"This is unacceptable! You need to leave, now."

"Hold on!"

"No, you hold on!" She grabbed his arm again. "Woah!"

The man tried pushing her off, and they both fell into the water.

He watched in darkness as they screamed at each other while trying to grab hold of the dock. The man had trouble holding himself afloat, apparently unable to swim. The woman struggled to help keep the man still. He quietly snuck his way onto the stairs, up and out of the door.

With relief he ran down the garden path, towards the side of the house where he felt two hands grab him. He felt the punch to his stomach and fell to the ground.

"You're a slippery little sucker, aren't you?" said the man who held him down. The same man that he had hit with the chair the night before.

CHAPTER 50

TIRED OF WAITING in the truck, Stef walked into the warehouse. Elena was on the phone at the far end of the space, walking around a pile of furniture just being unloaded from another truck.

"I was told these pieces would be strapped," she said in a curt tone. "Nothing here has been strapped, padded, or protected in any way. What kind of shipping is this?"

She held her hand up to Stef, signaling a short apology. Stef shrugged, letting her know it was fine, and looked at the pieces unloaded on the warehouse floor.

"We're going to have to review each piece and get back to you. Maybe one day delay," Elena replied to whomever she was speaking to, and then ended the call. "Sorry about this, Stef. I was expecting it to be packed in some way…this was just unexpected."

"That's OK. They're nice pieces."

"Yes, if you had come to see my window display at Sant' Ambrogio, you would have noticed them also at the villa event last night," she said to him, clearly disappointed he had not noticed. She didn't wait for his response. Instead, she turned back to the pieces and continued, "I was lucky with this one. The estate offloaded it almost immediately after the owner passed. I literally had two hours to go through the place and select what I wanted. Although, the client had a list of specific items he wanted. But I managed to get a few for my shop. I'm sure I missed out on some nice pieces, but I'm happy with what I've got." Elena carefully examined a tall metal lamp with hanging crystals. "I'm shocked this particular piece was not damaged."

Stef couldn't help but think the lamp looked familiar.

"Giulio," Elena called out to the foreman. "Where is the rest of the shipment? Bring it here, please. The couch. I want to see the couch."

Stef touched the crystal pendants, letting them clink against one another. Against the wall behind it lay a mirror haphazardly wrapped in brown bubble wrap.

"Oh! This was the first piece I selected." Elena snuck up behind him and gently removed the wrapping. "It wasn't on my client's list, but I wanted it. I had to fight another designer over it. But I charmed him into letting it go to me. Look at this brass frame – it's art deco." Elena caressed the mirror, examining it for scratches. "It goes on top of that table over there. Stef followed her eyes to a tall, narrow, white marble-topped table, which also looked familiar to him. He stared into the mirror and felt like something was not right, as if something was missing.

"Giulio, over here, please." Elena ran over to the large item Giulio and his men set down. It was a small, white sofa with large magenta flowers. "Stef, this is mine too. What do you think? Isn't it fantastic?"

Stef suddenly remembered why they all looked familiar.

"Elena, where did these come from?"

"I told you," she replied while caressing the sofa, which she was now sitting on. "From my latest acquisition…in Berlin."

"Berlin?" That was it!

"Yes," Elena picked at one of the flowers. "Damn it! I see a slight tear here. I noticed it loose when we displayed it in the window. I think I can fix that, though."

"Where in Berlin?" Stef looked back at the lamp. That was the lamp he had crashed into when he fell over onto that couch. And the mirror! That was the mirror in which he had admired his moustache – the thing that was missing.

"Oh, this beautiful apartment in Mitte," Elena replied as she jotted down notes. "The woman recently passed, and the estate was quick to rid of it all. When I was hired to go purchase specific items, I was also told there would be some available for me to purchase. When I heard that, I jumped at the chance to get my hands on some of the pieces. They were once featured in magazines…"

Stef stopped listening to Elena chatter about the quality of each piece and why she had added them to her Design Week display. It was all a very eerie coincidence. How had the furniture from the home he failed at burglarizing ended up with Elena? What were the odds? And the owner passed away? When? How?

"Passed away?" Stef asked.

"Yes, it happened about a week ago, maybe two? Earlier this month. Well, I'm not sure really, I don't remember the details. But I do know that sadly, she had been found a few days after passing." Elena waved her hand. "Or something to that matter, I don't know. They don't usually tell us all that."

Earlier this month, Stef repeated in his head. He was in that place not long ago. *What is going on?* A lot of this was too coincidental.

"Who is your client?" he asked her.

"Oh, I don't know the customer's name, but the man who hired me was…his name is on my paperwork at the office. I'd have to check." Elena continued to examine the sofa. "It's a new client. I'm hoping this works out and my name passes on."

Does Flavio have something to do with this? How does he know Elena? What is happening? Stef feared for Elena. How had she gotten caught up with Flavio? He needed to get in touch with Flavio and get to the bottom of it. And tell him to leave her the fuck alone.

"Giulio, I can't take any of these now." Elena filled a leather bag with small items. "I'm going to start with these, and will work on the rest when you deliver them tomorrow."

She removed a large tarp off a coffee table and continued to fill her bag with the decorative trinkets packed in a carton, one of which was a small wooden box with white flower carved on top. She looked inside and cocked her head.

"What is it?" Stef asked.

"What?" Elena replied as if she had forgotten he was there. "Oh. Nothing. I thought I remembered this box had something inside of it, something wrapped in a scarf. It must be back at the villa. I'll have to check when we get back to the city. I suppose I should take the box anyway. Why not?" She slipped the item into her bag. "Well, I guess we can go. Sorry for wasting your time with the truck and all."

"Oh, that's no problem." Stef opened the door for her. "I'm just glad you got to see the shipment."

"I'm going to let the client know we won't be delivering today, so maybe we can do lunch another time." Elena pulled out her phone and made the call. "Why don't you go bring the truck around and we'll just go back?"

"Just drop me at the shop," Elena instructed. "I'll see you tomorrow maybe? Help me deliver?"

He wanted to decline but could only bring himself to mutter "sure" in response.

"Good," Elena replied and tapped his cheek without any further emotion.

CHAPTER 51

SHE FELT HER tongue protruding from her mouth, and a spot of wet on her pillow confirmed she had drooled in her sleep. The sleeping pills really had done her in. The metallic buzz from the hallway continued to ring. Someone was determined to wake her and make her open the door. Suddenly remembering what had happened the night before, she sat up, wiped her mouth, and searched for her phone: eight missed calls from Stef.

She rolled out of bed, put on a robe, and shuffled to the monitor. In the corner of the screen, she saw Stef leaning on the door, pleading to himself for her to let him up.

"Come on, Beatrice," he whined. "Wake up. Open up."

She let out a long breath, buzzed him in, and unlocked her door. Stef blasted through.

"Beatrice!" He hugged her. "Beatrice, what happened to you?"

She didn't respond.

"You're trembling." He let go of his embrace and caressed her arms. "What happened to you last night? You left at some point. I couldn't find you."

She didn't know what to feel first. She wanted him to hug her again, tightly. But, at the same time, she wanted to slap him hard. She hugged him and sobbed into his shoulder.

"Beatrice," Stef caressed her head. "It's OK. I'm here. What can I do for you? What's wrong?"

"I was almost killed last night!" She let it all out in one big breath, then sobbed again.

"What are you talking about?"

"I was followed." Her phrases came out in between sobs. "It was foggy. I could barely see. It was dark. And I was followed. Some strange man. He chased me."

"Who?"

"I don't know!" She pushed him away. "I can't even begin to tell you how scared I was. I don't want to even know what he was planning to do with me."

"I'm so sorry, Beatrice." Stef pulled out one of the kitchen chairs. "Why don't you sit down? Tell me what happened."

She didn't want to follow his suggestion, but truthfully she was happy someone – especially him – was with her at that moment. She took the seat. He sat across from her and held her hand.

"It's OK." He cupped her hand. "What happened?"

"I don't know, really. I left the party—"

"When? Why did you leave?"

"I just left," she replied shortly, lying. "I was outside having a cigarette." She didn't want him to know he was the cause of her leaving. She'd rather he think she was just taking a break outside.

"And?"

"The fog was ridiculously thick; it had worsened since we got to the party." She fumbled on her kitchen table, looking for a pack of cigarettes. "I was about to light my cigarette when I saw a man approaching me." She dropped the pile of papers, no pack to be found.

"This man," Stef coaxed her to continue. "Did he threaten you?"

"Yes. Well, no. But he followed me." She got up and looked around her kitchen for the cigarettes. Where had she left them? "I walked over to the tram stop, to check the late night times, and he followed me. I wasn't sure he was following me then. I felt maybe that he was. So, I continued down the street and saw that he was, in fact, following me."

"Where were you going?"

"I don't know," she lied. "I was just walking. The point is, he was following me. The fog was so thick, I could barely see in front of me. But I could hear his footsteps behind me. Anyway, I kept taking odd turns, and he continued after me. At one point he grabbed my arm and I screamed."

"My goodness, Beatrice." Stef reached for her arm and held her hand as she stood in the doorway to the living room. "Why didn't you just come back?"

"I wasn't thinking." She sat back down. "I was afraid, so I ran. I ran towards the lights, thinking they would lead me to a busy area like Piazza Duomo. Anyway, at one point I noticed the man had a gun." She paused and sobbed again.

"A gun?!" Stef stood up and started to pace. "Go on."

"I didn't know what to do, Stef. So I ran and he ran after me."

Stef held her again with a tight embrace, feeling her body tremble as she spoke.

"What did he do to you?" he whispered.

"Nothing," she continued, letting Stef go and walking into the living room. Stef followed. "I didn't know where to run. I found myself in some random street near the Galleria. I hid in doorways, in the shadows, but he continued to pursue me. Eventually, he pushed me into an elevator and we fought inside."

"Fought?!" Stef stood still in shock. "You mean you were attacked?"

"Yes!"

"My god." Stef wiped his face in horror. "How did you get away?"

"I don't know. My defenses just kicked in."

"And you didn't even call me? I would have helped you."

"I didn't think. I wasn't thinking. I just wanted to survive." Beatrice stood straight in shock with the memory of what had transpired next.

"Beatrice?" Stef approached her, but she shook him off. "Beatrice, what happened?"

"He fell."

"What?"

"I pushed, and he fell. Just like that, he fell."

"Wait a minute." Stef pulled the newspaper out of his pocket. "Was this him?"

She looked at the newspaper and quickly scanned the article. The man was known by police, had previous trouble with law. He had been inactive for quite some time. There may have been a woman fleeing from the scene, but no concrete reports or evidence.

Her face must have had a look of horror, because Stef led her to the couch and caressed her arms again.

"Beatrice," he called to her softly. "Beatrice, was that you?"

She nodded in silence. She walked over to her coat and searched her pocket for the cigarettes, only to be horrified again.

"What is it?" Stef walked over to her. "Beatrice, what is it?"

Beatrice felt the bracelet inside the coat pocket. She had forgotten she had taken it. She was embarrassed. She wanted to confess but was too ashamed to admit her reason for doing such a childish thing. She looked away from Stef. He rubbed her arm as she pulled out the cigarette pack, leaving the bracelet inside the pocket.

"I think it was him, Stef," she continued, shaking while she pulled out a cigarette. "I couldn't really tell. I looked in his eyes. I think it was him. I think Kevin was after me." After five tries, she finally lit the cigarette.

"Beatrice."

"It was him," she continued. "That Kevin. It had to be. I saw him at the party. He saw me. He wanted to kill me."

"Beatrice—"

"It was him!"

"It wasn't him."

"Yes, it was." She paced the room, nervously puffing at the cigarette. "He followed me. He pulled out a gun. But he didn't shoot me. Why?"

"It wasn't him."

"Yes, it was."

"No, it wasn't."

"How would you know?" she snapped. She wanted to spit in his face. She wanted to call him out for sneaking into the room with Elena. He had no idea what he was talking about. Because while this was all happening, he was on top of Elena. "You weren't there," she added. "I don't know where you were."

"It wasn't him," Stef insisted. "I know because I finally saw him."

"Yes, Stef. I saw him too. And he saw me. He knew I was there, and when he saw me leave, he followed me." Beatrice squashed her half smoked cigarette into the green glass ashtray and pulled out a new one. "He wanted to kill me. That must be his plan, Stef. He's back, and he's planning to kill us both. What have we done?"

"Beatrice—"

"What have you done?" she screamed. "You got me into this mess! You did this. And because of you, I was almost killed last night!" She stood in shock again. "Oh my god…Because of you, I killed a man!"

"Beatrice, it wasn't him," Stef repeated. "I was with him last night. We were all looking for you. Me, Kevin, and Elena. We saw Kevin downstairs…Beatrice…they know each other."

"What?"

"Kevin and Elena," Stef repeated. "They knew each other. They are acquaintances. She introduced me to him – well, reintroduced. Of course, we explained that we had met at the bar, but she knew him. And not only did she know him, she embraced him, kissed him on the cheek, and locked her arm in his."

Beatrice couldn't find the words to respond. How did they know each other? Had they known each other all along? Did she and Stef dump a friend of Elena? And did he know that she and

Stef were the ones to throw him into the river? And if he wasn't the one who followed her, then who was the man that she killed?

"I don't understand."

"You're telling me." Stef dropped onto the couch. "This is all so confusing. And it's getting dangerous. We need to do something. We need to stop this. All of it."

"Stop what exactly? We don't even know what the hell is going on?" Beatrice dropped her unlit cigarette, walked into the bathroom, and splashed water onto her face.

"Kevin knows Elena," Stef said aloud. "And I don't know how long they've known each other. I mean, if they knew each other this whole time, I would assume Kevin would have told her about us. About the river. Unless Kevin doesn't realize it was us."

"What are you going on about?" Beatrice returned from the bathroom, wiping her face with a face towel.

"I don't think he knows who we are."

"What do you mean?" Beatrice let the towel hang in her hand.

"He saw us at the bar, correct?"

"Correct."

"The bar where...the *incident* happened."

"Yes?"

"When he returned, he saw you, Beatrice, behind that same bar."

"Yes..."

"Don't you see, Bea? He didn't recognize you. He didn't recognize me! He doesn't know!"

"Stef, if he doesn't know, then who the hell was trying to kill me last night?" Saying the words aloud hit her every time. She held the back of the armchair and cried. "Stef, I may not have killed the man we dumped into the river. But I killed a man last night! My god, I'm a murderer!"

"Stop it." He stood up and held her. "Stop saying that. You were only defending yourself. You're not a murderer."

"A man is dead because of me."

"You were defending yourself." He said it again, softly. He embraced her, kissed her, and repeated. "You were only defending yourself."

She fell into his embrace.

"Come on." He held her hand. "Shower up. Get dressed."

"What?"

"We're going to get a drink."

"Are you crazy? Did you not hear what I just told you?"

"I'm not leaving you here alone." Stef led her to the bathroom. "Besides, you're going to want to come with me."

"I can't go, Stef." She adjusted her robe.

"Why not?"

"I think I need to go to the police."

"Hell, no!" He held her arms. "Are you crazy? You cannot do that. We have no idea who that guy was. And they have no connection to you."

"But that's just it." She removed his hands, pushed him out of the bathroom, and turned on the shower. "Don't you see?" She called out to him. "That man was following me from the party."

"So?" He replied as he looked around her room.

"So, someone there must have seen us leaving. Sooner or later, it will all come out."

"So, wait for later." Stef opened the third drawer of the bureau and selected a pair of underpants and a bra. "Why go turn yourself in like you're some criminal? You're not."

"Don't say that," Beatrice said from the shower. "I just want this to be over with. All of it."

"Well, no offense, Beatrice," Stef peeped into the bathroom. "But, you go to the police, it will only be the beginning."

Silence.

"Just come get a drink, a quick aperitivo." Stef went back to setting her clothes on the bed. He didn't know what the hell she would want to wear, but he felt if he put something out, it would prod her to get dressed or pull something else from her closet. "And we'll sort it all out. Then when we get back, we'll know what to do."

Beatrice rinsed the lather from her body, turned off the shower, and toweled dry.

"It's only an aperitivo," Stef continued. "We'll be back before you know it." He reached for her closet door and opened it for her.

Beatrice emerged from the bathroom and found him going through her rack of dresses. He examined every one and pulled out the shortest black dress she had.

"No." She pulled the dress from his hands and hung it back in the closet, then pulled out a green one. He smiled.

"I'm really frightened, Stef."

"I know." He kissed her on the forehead and left the room. "I will not let anything happen to you. We'll meet him for a drink, and then we'll be done. I promise."

"Meet?" Beatrice said back. "What do you mean, 'meet him'?"

"Oh," Stef peeped into the room. "Didn't I mention? We're meeting Kevin."

"What?"

"The stranger," Stef repeated from the living room. "Kevin."

"What?!"

CHAPTER 52

Kevin

SOMETIMES YOU JUST have to let the sadness happen. When it hits you, it just hits you. You could be having a grand old time – days or weeks go by and all is normal – then one day, you wake up with the company of melancholy. You can't control it. It just comes and surrounds you. Strangely, its embrace is like a warm blanket wrapped around you, comforting you as you lay in bed or on the couch, just feeling the sadness, like a drug.

You want out of the sadness, but you've tried every method of distraction. You watch a comedic film or TV series, read a nonsense fluff book, listen to peppy music, bake, yoga, gym, but you know at the other end of those distracting tasks, sadness is patiently waiting for you. You also try phoning friends – ones that are a guaranteed laugh – but sometimes those friends are not available. And deep down, you can't rely on others to get you out of the sadness.

Sadness doesn't just come overnight. It visits at any time. You can have a fine day, get home to your empty apartment, sit on your plush sofa, and suddenly feel it coming over you. You feel the tears sliding down your cheeks, that comfort of sadness.

Although you don't want it to take over, you cannot stop it from doing so. Eventually, you avoid people and phone calls; cancel invites, even. After a while, your acquaintances stop calling and you're left with fewer people with whom to socialize, fewer reasons to get out of the house.

What is most annoying in all of this is that you know you need to find something to prevent sadness from coming back. Sometimes you believe yourself to be weak when you let it take over.

And one day you finally decide to make a change. That maybe that is what you need in your boring life. So, you find yourself doing something irrational. You book a flight to Europe – a change of scenery may help knock sadness to the curb. Europe sounds nice. A few days of strolling along the Seine would maybe boost your mood. So, you pack a small bag and just leave.

You don't tell anyone; you don't feel you have to, really. Besides, you let yourself believe that no one really cares – I mean *really* cares. And even if they did care, you have already decided you don't care about them. It's not about them. You need to fix you.

This sadness thing has been going on for far too long. The secret side of you that no one really knows, cares to know, or you did not allow to let be known. You are tired of carrying sadness and its brutally heavy burden. Maybe you just need something new in your life; new scenery, new people, or just a whole new life. Or maybe it was time to just put an end to it all – an official end to the life you have.

You phone the office and tell them you have to leave for a few days – a family emergency. They are sorry for whatever it is and encourage you to take all the time you need. On your way to the airport, the phone buzzes with texts from acquaintances that missed out on you last night, hoping you're feeling well and can't wait to tell you what you missed. The taxi is stuck in traffic on the bridge out of the city. The phone continues to buzz. You roll down the window and chuck it into the river below. You're done. You watch the expensive phone flip through the air and splash into the dirty water. Plop.

And just like that, Kevin had left his sad life.

CHAPTER 53

WHEN HE HAD finally gotten to Milan, Kevin selected a hotel with no special view. He had no idea how long he would be staying in the city, so it really hadn't mattered. It had been three days now, and he regretted taking this excursion, prolonging his first mission. Why had he agreed to even listen to the stranger in Paris? Maybe Kevin was looking for something to show him that ending his life was a bad decision. Maybe Kevin was looking for a reason to continue. Maybe he was wrong.

The hotel room was still dark, with spots of sunlight trickling in from the slim cracks of the blinds. The air was stale, warm, and slightly suffocating. It was a struggle, but the only reason Kevin thought of getting out of the bed that morning was to let in some fresh air.

Curmudgeonly, he rolled onto his left side, not bothering to save the soft pillow as it fell onto the carpeted floor. He again lay flat, hoping to ignore the heavy heat surrounding him. It didn't work. He moaned and kicked the wrinkled sheet off of his right leg. Still, he had no desire to get up from the bed. He kicked again – this time with both legs – and managed to swing them around to the side of the mattress. They hung there – bent at the knees – as the rest of his body remained flat on the bed. It was like a safe haven to remain attached to that mattress and those wrinkled sheets, which had comforted him through the night.

He lay there, staring at the ceiling, trying to get lost in his thoughts, hoping to, once again, ignore the uncomfortable heat and the thin lines of sunlight that annoyingly beckoned him to rise. Realizing there was no fighting the morning, he finally swung his bottom half in the air and kicked his upper body off the bed, landing with his feet on the soft carpet.

He stood slouching and shuffled to the window – he needed that fresh spring air. Slowly, he pulled the chain, allowing the sunlight to burst through the blinds, and more heat along with it. His eyes adjusted to the light as he reached for the latch and opened the window. Immediately, the cool air blew into the room, tickling his body, while Kevin breathed in, filling his lungs. It went through his nostrils and soothed his air passages, washing his lungs. Ahh, fresh air.

He straightened his back, stretched his arms towards the ceiling, and yawned. He stretched his torso to the left, then to the right. He reached his arms over his head towards the north wall, then again to the south. His eyes were now fully open, and his mind begged for coffee. It was time to clean up and begin his day.

He looked at his watch laying on the desk just in front of him: 07:02 AM. It was still early, but Kevin was never one to sleep in anyway. As much as he tried to do it, his body – or maybe it was his mind – just would not cooperate. The warm front was still sweeping through the city. Springtime in the city was just perfect. Disappointed with his failure to sleep through his day,

Kevin made his way into the bathroom, took a long, relieving piss, and jumped into a cold, refreshing shower.

He padded himself dry, put on the hotel robe, and walked over to the door. The morning paper had been slid underneath. He picked up the newspaper and threw it onto the desk without even looking at it.

The cool breeze continued to clean the air in the room. Kevin stretched his arms again and noticed his body in the oversized mirror. His focus was on the slightly flabby belt encircling his midsection – the overt sign of love handles. When had this happened to his body? The reflection was another cringe-worthy reminder that his youth was trickling away. He did not like getting older, but did anyone, really?

Defeated by his fading physique, he swung his upper body left to right, like he used to do at the gym. He straightened his back and reached his left arm down to his right foot, then his right arm to his left foot. 1-2-3-4-5. He counted out loud as he performed each move. He felt less heavy. He was content and satisfied with his small accomplishment of actually doing something that was good for himself. He continued. The old routine was coming back to him. Next, he performed five lunges on each leg. Then, he lay on his back for five sit-ups. He followed that by flipping over and struggling to complete five push-ups.

He hadn't done physical activity like that for over two years. At that time, he had been a member of a mediocre fitness facility and was able to do more than just five of each task. He considered this morning's routine a restart to a new morning ritual: simple exercises just to get the blood flowing and boost his mood – words his doctor kept telling him as he crossed the threshold of middle age. His body felt rejuvenated and refreshed to have bent his joints and stretched his muscles again. For another brief moment, Kevin had forgotten that he wanted his days to end.

Content with his exercise ritual, Kevin went back into the bathroom, brushed his teeth, fixed his hair, and examined his face for any unshaven stubble. All clean. He looked at his reflection and smiled. Today is going to be a good day, he thought to himself. He winked at his reflection, swung around on his heels, and skipped to the armoire.

He put on his favorite casual blue slacks, camel colored leather belt, and white button down. No matter how low he felt, or how content, he always took pride on how he looked. He always dressed well – it just made him feel worthy.

He was motivated to leave the room. Otherwise, he would have spent the day lying in bed wallowing in sadness and misery. He reminded himself that he didn't come all the way to Europe to spend his final days in a dark room. Sure, Paris was supposed to be where it was going to end. But circumstances led him to Milan, a slight distraction, a moment of forgetting the idea, but the feelings had returned. When he had met Elena that late night near Sant'Ambrogio, he thought that maybe she came into his life as a sign that he could start anew. But then the sadness came back to remind him why he was in Europe in the first place; it was time for it all to end.

Last night, at the event, Elena had formally introduced him to her handsome friend Stef. Kevin thought he looked familiar but couldn't quite place him. When Elena had slid her arm under Kevin's elbow as she introduced her friend, Kevin remembered thinking, *Maybe Elena could be a door to a new life?* This morning, though, he woke up with the heavy burden of sadness reminding him it would not go away.

At breakfast, he mindlessly sipped his coffee and prodded at the pastry in front of him. He had originally intended to taste a slice of Milan's famous panettone, but he decided on this one based on the server's suggestion. She explained the pastry chef was from Verona and it was a specialty of that city. It was called *la torta Russa* – or the Russian torte. The name of the cake implied the shape of the recognizable hat worn by Russian Cossack military, as he had seen in one of his favorite films, *Dr. Zhivago*.

He took a bite of the cake, which filled his mouth with a rich and dense almond flavored delight. Soon after, his grey cloud caught up with him. The sadness crept back in through the crevices of content. Kevin knew it hadn't returned; it had never left. In fact, it was always there, waiting to come to the forefront.

He focused on the Russian torte again, allowing him to momentarily shake the sadness away. But when he looked at the empty seat across from him, the sadness struck him again. He was alone. Not only was he alone at the breakfast table, he was alone in life. He had abandoned everyone he knew. He had decided he was done. He promised himself not to be distracted from his final, life-ending mission.

After breakfast, he wandered through the neighborhood finding himself drawn to two tall buildings with greenery hanging from the balconies. He had remembered them from his guidebook as the famous Vertical Gardens. He walked through a park of zig-zagged pathways lined with trees, then up the steps into piazza Gae Aulenti. The rain began to fall, forcing him into a café where he sat with another cup of coffee.

One of the servers quietly approached him with his hands clasped and offered him another coffee. Kevin took longer than needed to respond, and finally agreed to another cup. He sat back against the plush yellow pillow and looked out the window. The stone of the modern piazza glistened with droplets of rain that continued to fall.

He had to figure out how and where he would do it. In Paris, he had planned to just drop himself into the river Seine. As he thought about that idea again, he realized it wasn't a guaranteed ending. He had to come up with another way. He looked out the window, watching the people rush to work maybe. If he recalled correctly, piazza Aulenti was surrounded by commercial buildings, so, yes, these people were most likely going to work.

The server returned with a warm cup of caffe Americano.

"Pardon," Kevin asked. "Do you know when this rain is supposed to stop?"

"Oh, it's only supposed to be like this for the morning. Welcome to Milan." The server said it almost sarcastically, then added, "I like the rain, don't you? Rain seems to enrich the colors of everything around you. Just look at the deep grey color of the piazza. Look how rich it appears now with the shine of the wet rain, like a varnish, like on a canvas."

"Well, that's a beautiful way to look at rain. You must be an artist."

"Yes, I am. And yes, it is," the server replied and walked away, not allowing any time for Kevin to respond. Instead, he turned to new guests that had just entered the café.

CHAPTER 54

SINCE THE TRIP with Elena earlier in the day, Stef quietly tried piecing together how Elena was connected to Berlin, or to Flavio. He worried for her. All day he couldn't get his mind off of what could happen to her in the hands of Flavio and his goons. He kept this discovery from Beatrice, not wanting to worry her even more after her dangerous ordeal last night. He was startled by the flick of Beatrice's lighter sparking up her cigarette. The smoke soon clouded his face.

"Are you serious?" he seethed and waved the smoke away.

"What?" Beatrice looked at him, annoyed. "We're just sitting here, and I was getting anxious."

Stef shook his head past her, indicating for her to move and smoke away from him. He hated the smell of cigarette smoke on him. Especially when he was dressed in his favorite grey sports jacket. Beatrice rolled her eyes and walked away from him, further into the darkness.

"Beatrice!" Stef called out to her as softly as he could. "Beatrice. There he is. Across the street, waiting for the tram." She put out her cigarette and joined Stef.

"What tram is that?" he whispered. "Which one goes by here? Number one, right?"

"Why are we following him?" she asked. "He knows where to meet us."

"I want to see what he's like," Stef replied. "If this Kevin really is Kevin. Or is he some imposter? Let's just observe him for a bit and see what he does."

He pulled Beatrice along, keeping themselves hidden by shuffling among the other people also waiting for the tram.

"This is making no sense, Stef," Beatrice whispered. "Where is all this coming from? You did make plans to meet him tonight, did you not?"

"Well…," Stef replied. "Sort of, not really. He seemed a little put off by me."

"You didn't hit on him again, did you?"

"No! God, no," Stef replied unassumingly.

"Oh god, Stef. What the hell are you up to?"

"Shh, just follow my lead."

Stef occasionally snuck a peek at Kevin – or the imposter – who at that moment was engrossed in reading some sort of document. He finally looked again and noticed that the document was a map. Kevin folded the map, turned around, and walked down the street behind him.

"Where is he going?" Stef asked as he pulled Beatrice, who was hooked under his arm. They kept their distance following Kevin. "He had a map again," Stef added.

"A what?" Beatrice was trying to step quietly so as to not cause attention.

"A map. He must have been looking for a different tram, maybe? Where is he going?"

Kevin turned left down a well-lit street, then turned right down an even busier street, where he stopped at a different tram stop, waiting for the number two.

"These shoes are killing me," Beatrice whined, trying to slow Stef down.

"Well, why did you wear those strappy things? You knew our plan for tonight."

"Stef! We were going to have a drink, or an aperitivo, as you said. I thought I should at least look the part." She stopped, adjusting her shoe strap.

"Well, you overdressed," Stef replied. "I mean, you look incredible, but you overdid it." He knew it was a quick save and hoped Beatrice didn't notice. She ignored him and continued their light pursuit.

"Why couldn't this guy just take the closest metro?" Beatrice ignored his useless compliment. "Where is he going?"

They were getting too close to Kevin. Stef pulled her in and caressed her cheek. She looked at him confused.

"I'm just making us look like we belong on the street," Stef explained. "He can't see our faces. I don't want him to know we're following him." He then added, "Just take the shoes off."

Beatrice looked at him in silence. She wanted to slap him. But as she looked at him under the streetlights, she was reminded of his handsomeness. She closed her eyes, feeling the back of his hand on her cheek. She breathed in his cologne; it had a scent of wood and man. She wanted to kiss him right there. When Stef pulled her along and out of the moment, she again wanted to slap him.

CHAPTER 55

AS THEY WALKED along the grand canal, Stef kept trying to run all the pieces in his mind. Flavio hired a stranger to steal the bracelet in Berlin. The items in Berlin were somehow with Elena. The stranger, whom he and Beatrice had dumped into the Po, seemed to have returned and was coincidentally at Elena's villa party. In fact, he – whom they now knew as Kevin – appeared to have been somewhat acquainted with Elena. How? Was their meeting just a coincidence? The villa where Elena had coincidently had her latest furniture acquisition on display. The furniture that coincidentally had come from the same apartment Stef had tried to steal from in Berlin. That same apartment where Flavio's new man – maybe this Kevin – had apparently succeeded in burglarizing, but was somehow now missing. Flavio had also mentioned this man had stolen from him. Stef assumed Flavio was implying the piece that was missing – the bracelet. After accusing Stef of being in cahoots with the stranger – who might be this Kevin – Flavio asked Stef to help him find the man who may have been working with the stranger. Wait! Was there a third man? Was the Kevin in the river a third man? Is this Kevin not the Kevin in the river? Or was this man the Kevin? Was this Kevin the man Flavio had hired?

This Kevin knew Elena, so maybe he was connected to Flavio? Or maybe river Kevin was the a different man, working with the man that Flavio had hired. But where was that man? Was there another man? Or was Kevin the missing man? Confused, Stef shook himself out of his thoughts.

"Stef, are you listening to me?" Beatrice stopped their stride. "What is going on with you? Speak up."

"I'm sorry, Bea." Stef put his head on her shoulder. "I've just got a lot on my mind right now."

Beatrice couldn't help but think Stef's melancholy was caused by his morning with the selfish Elena. She rolled her eyes and continued their pace.

"Here." Stef turned to the left. "The place is just in here."

"Poison Ivy?" Beatrice read the sign aloud. "Are you sure he'll be here?"

"Yes, I had suggested it to him," Stef replied while opening the door, causing the jungle beats to trickle out into the street. "Come on. He promised he would come."

"And there he is," Beatrice replied. "My god, I don't know if I can do this."

"Relax." He rubbed her back. "We've got this."

Kevin had been sitting at one of the small, round bamboo tables in the center of the room. The walls decorated with tribal masks and spears heightening the tiki jungle theme of Poison Ivy – the bar could have been decorated by the seductive comic book villain. All around the space were assortments of oversized green plants ranging from Birds of Paradise, Dracaena, Banana Leaf trees, and ferns, all reaching out to the patrons that brushed by. The lighting was dark red and orange hues accentuated by occasion spirals of yellow and violet along the walls.

An oversized bamboo branch stretched along the bar that was shaped like a tiki hut. The staff wore moss green vests and painted black lines across their eyes, resembling the mask of a racoon.

"May we join you?" Stef sat in the chair next to Kevin before he could respond.

CHAPTER 56

THE SERVER PLACED a Mai Tai, a Pearl Diver, and a Navy Grog – down on the table and left when the party told them they wouldn't be needing anything further for the moment. Kevin, Stef, and Beatrice stared at each other as they each sipped their sweet and potent concoctions.

The server returned with a tray of bar snacks – spicy cashews, sticks of chicken, and pineapple herb crackers. Stef immediately reached for the chicken and smiled at Kevin. Kevin, still unsure of the encounter, reached for the cashews. Beatrice adjusted herself in the throne-like bamboo seat and leaned in.

"No, my name is not Rosaline," she replied to Kevin's confused inquiry. "I'm sorry about that."

Kevin was disappointed. He sat back, offered a smile, and popped another cashew in his mouth.

"Kevin," Beatrice spoke again after some silence. "Speaking of names, we have something to tell you." She looked back and forth at both of them.

"What's that?" Kevin replied mid chew. He tried to keep his calm, not show any sense that he felt somewhat uncomfortable. And he didn't know why.

"Well, actually, we have a question for you," she added.

Stef glared at her, but she ignored him.

"OK." Kevin was intrigued.

"Who are you?" she blurted.

Stef choked on his drink.

"Are you OK?" Kevin patted him on the back.

"Huh?" Stef coughed. "Oh, yes. I'm fine. Thank you. Sorry."

"I mean, really," Beatrice continued. "Kevin, tell us who you are."

"What?" Kevin replied. "I don't know what you mean."

Beatrice smiled at him, sat back, and sipped her drink. Stef glared at her again. She wanted to slap him. She leaned in again and decided to just say it.

"We know you're not Kevin Benton. We know you are pretending to be him and we don't know why. Is there something we should know about you or about Kevin? Are you an imposter?"

"What? I am Kevin Benton." Kevin sat up, unsure if he should stand up and leave. He put his drink down on the table.

"Kevin," Stef put his hand out. "Sorry for the abruptness. You can be honest with us. We won't tell anyone."

"What are you talking about?"

"Why are you doing this to us?" Beatrice shouted. She had had enough. "What do you want from us?! Who are you?!" She sat back shaking.

Stef gently caressed Beatrice's arms to calm her. "Beatrice, you need cigarette."

"No, I don't." Beatrice forcefully pulled her arms away. "Stop touching me."

"Beatrice." Stef repeated her name as if she knew better. "Beatrice, OK, maybe not a cigarette. Or how about you grab us another round?"

Beatrice breathed out and nodded in agreement. She needed to step away. The whole situation was getting to her. The fear of getting caught was growing more and more inside of her. Was Kevin the man they had dumped into the river? She had to know. And why had he returned? What did he want? She didn't know how much more she could take. She walked away from them and over to the bar. She sat down and ordered herself a drink.

"What is going on?" Kevin stood up too.

"Kevin." Stef sat back down, gesturing for Kevin to join him. "Please, allow me to explain."

"Please do."

"We know you're not Kevin."

"I am Kevin! What are you talking about?!"

"Please relax. Let me explain."

The server appeared and dropped another round. "From your lady friend." He gave a sly smirk, indicating that one – if not both – of the men would probably get lucky with the lady tonight. Stef proffered a fake smile, took a sip, and continued as the waiter walked away.

"We met a man a few weeks ago – at the bar where Beatrice was tending. He came in towards the end of the night and kept ordering drink after drink. As the bar emptied, the man stayed in his seat and continued to drink. He was not in his right mind at that point, as you can understand." Stef paused and took another sip.

"Well?" Kevin was losing his patience, wondering where Stef was going with his story

"Well, not long after that, the man went missing." Stef didn't want to say more, in the usual attempt to keep himself and Beatrice distant from the death.

"I don't understand."

"He was found dead, Kevin."

"Dead?"

"Yes, dead." Stef took another sip.

Kevin picked up his drink and sipped in confusion.

"I still don't understand what you're telling me." Kevin sat back in his seat, indicating he was not leaving.

"He went by the name of Kevin Benton."

"What?"

"The man tried to use his credit card at the bar. On it was his name: Kevin Benton." Stef reached for his drink again and continued with the story – the alibi version of it. "Unfortunately, the card didn't work, so he paid with cash…a little more cash than he needed to, really. He just threw it on the bar." Stef controlled himself with the details. He didn't want to say more than he needed to.

"Wait a minute." Kevin sat back. "That must have been the man who stole my wallet."

"What?"

"I was in Paris before coming here to Milan," explained Kevin. "I, well, you don't need to know why I was there, but I was there. Anyway, I was expected to come to Milan earlier than I had, to meet someone. But when I was on the train, I found that my wallet was missing, so it altered my trip. Instead, I first had to sort out the credit cards and identification.

"After all that was finally sorted," Kevin finally pulled the umbrella out of his cocktail, then continued, "it took longer than I wanted it to. Anyway, even though I had already missed the appointment I had." He looked up in shock and said, "Which was at some odd address of a bar – where your friend Rosaline – I mean, Beatrice – was tending." He put his glass down and said to himself aloud, "He must have seen the note in my wallet and gone for the appointment himself. But why?"

"What are you talking about?" Stef leaned in.

"I had an appointment, as I mentioned, in Milan, with…" Kevin stopped his sentence, not wanting to give more details. "Well, anyway, as I explained, I didn't make the appointment – I was held up with security sorting out my identification and credit card situation."

"Right…"

"Well, the man – the one you met – clearly had stolen my wallet and inside found my note to myself with the appointment time and address. But if he stole my wallet, then why would he want to be in a place where I would need to be? He didn't have…Why risk getting caught? Makes no sense."

"No, it doesn't," Stef replied. "He didn't have what?"

"Wait!" Kevin was beginning to slur his words. He was drunk. "Hold on. If this other man's dead…was he murdered? If so, by whom? And was the killer coming after me? Why? Is my life in danger?"

"I don't think so. I think you're OK. But I guess we first need to know who he was."

"I don't know. All I know is that I went to the hotel that I had booked originally for that time, and when I checked in…" Kevin stopped talking. It was beginning to make sense. He continued, laying out the possible happenings aloud to himself too. "When I checked in, the front desk person welcomed me back and asked me if I received my belongings. Now, at the time, it didn't occur to me what she was asking. I just assumed it was a barrier with the English language. I assumed that when she welcomed be back, she had seen me before – or thought she had – and she was referring to the bag I was traveling with, but maybe she meant other belongings?"

"What do you mean?"

"I mean, by 'other belongings' I wonder if she meant the bag that belonged to this man that maybe you met – the dead man."

"Wait. You think his stuff is at your hotel?"

"Well, I don't know, but that's probably what she meant. If she thought *I* was the same person, that is."

Stef's heart was racing. Could anything in the stuff belonging to the man incriminate him or Beatrice? Was there a trace that would connect him to the two of them? He began to sweat. And then another thought popped into his head: How was this connected to Flavio?

"Are you OK?" asked Kevin, who continued to suck on the straw in his empty drink.

"What? Oh, yes. Yes, sorry." Stef finished off his drink and waved for the waiter to send over two more.

"I don't understand," Stef blurted. He didn't want to mention Flavio, or Elena, or the connection yet. He didn't want this Kevin imposter to know he was connected to Flavio.

"What don't you understand?"

Stef had to divert the question. He didn't know what to do. He tried throwing out another one to keep this man on his story. He picked up his third Navy Grog and asked, "You were saying. That night, you checked into the hotel…"

"Well, after checking in," Kevin continued. "I went up to my room, showered, and slept – it was late."

"OK…" Stef was relieved that the man continued his story.

"The next morning, I got up, dressed, and went out for a walk, got my coffee…" Kevin was retracing his steps out loud, clearly putting it all together for the first time as he was talking very loudly. The cocktails had clearly had an effect on his volume.

"Yes? Yes…"

"Well, when I returned, the person at the front desk – it was a different person this time, the morning crew."

"Yes, right. OK…" Stef waved his hand trying to wipe away the irrelevant details.

"That new person wished me 'good morning' and said I had a message. And he handed me an envelope. I took the envelope upstairs – I had to rush upstairs because I had to go the restroom really bad. Anyway, I did my thing, then showered. I had forgotten about the envelope. When I got out of the shower, I saw the envelope I had thrown on the bed. I opened it to find a note to meet again at Sant'Ambrogio that evening. With it was another note that said, *Sorry I missed you. Hope to see you this evening.* And it baffled me. How did she know where to find me?"

"Who?!" Stef couldn't stand Kevin's slow delivery. Maybe the Navy Grogs had wiped out his filter. Sure, Kevin was just now figuring it out, but Stef realizing this had to be Elena. He didn't want it to be but he wanted Kevin to say it already.

"When I got to Sant'Ambrogio, who do I find working in a window? The woman I was told to meet by the man in Paris!" Kevin scoffed still in disbelief of the coincidence. He took another sip and added, "The woman whose appointment I had missed."

"What?" Stef was confused. All of Kevin's answers had just caused Stef so many more questions. If Elena was the person who was supposed to meet this Kevin that night, why did she not ever come into the bar? *Wait*, thought Stef, *then who the hell was that man at the bar?*

"Kevin…" Stef said his name slowly as he thought it through.

"Yeah?" Kevin stirred the straw of his third Pearl Diver and sucked it down while Stef was entranced in his own thoughts.

"You were supposed to meet Elena at the bar?"

"Well, no…maybe. I suppose so. I was never really told who it was. I assumed it was a man."

"This man you mentioned. He's the one that told you? The man in Paris…," Stef said slowly, trying to straighten out Kevin's confusing story.

"Yes?"

"*He* was supposed to meet you at the bar?"

"Well, yeah. I mean, I'm not sure, really. All I know is that I was supposed to make the drop at that bar. That was the original plan."

"But Elena, nor the man, never came into the bar that night," Stef declared, assuming the man may have been Flavio. Soon after, he realized he sounded as if he was sure of it.

"Not when I was there. Or are you talking about the original night?" Kevin slurred. "Wait. What night are you talking about?"

"The original night that the real Kevin…I mean, the other Kevin, imposter Kevin, or I-don't-know-who-the-fuck-he-was-Kevin, had come in. The night of your original appointment."

"The man I was supposed to meet wasn't there?" Kevin repeated. "Wait. How would you know who I was supposed to meet?"

"No." Stef needed to cover it up. He quickly added, "I mean, I assume he hadn't come because the other Kevin was alone all night."

"Well, now that's odd. Unless he couldn't make it to the appointment either. I don't know." Kevin shrugged, put down his empty glass, and ate a cracker.

"Well, aren't you concerned?"

"About what?"

"This other Kevin?"

"Not really, I mean, other than wonder why – well, I have no idea why he'd go to the appointment. Unless, he was the man I was to meet? But that doesn't make sense." Kevin was definitely drunk. He had completely forgotten about the possibility that this other Kevin was probably the man who stole his wallet and the probability that his life was in jeopardy.

"Exactly," Stef continued. "And what did he leave behind at the hotel?"

"Oh! Maybe my wallet!"

With that, Stef's fear of getting caught came back. He surely wasn't going to tell this Kevin that he and Beatrice had disposed of the wallet in question. He decided to just let that thought float away.

"Wait!" Kevin sat up again, still slurring his words. "Who is trying to kill me?"

"Kill you?" Stef flustered his response. "No one. I mean, why would anyone want to kill you? Have you done something to make someone want to kill you?"

"So, Elena's safe?"

"Safe? I mean, she's harmless. What does she have to do with all of this?"

"I just know I had to give her what I was supposed to deliver."

"And what was that?"

Beatrice finally left the seat at the bar and rejoined the guys.

"You're drunk," she said to Stef disappointingly, with her arms on her hips. "And you got him drunk."

"I didn't get him drunk," Stef replied. "He got drunk on his own."

"I saw you order more drinks."

"Beatrice…"

"It doesn't matter now." Beatrice grabbed his arm. "We have to go."

"Hold on." Stef tried squirming out of her grasp. "We're not done talking here."

"No," Beatrice squeezed his arm tighter. "We have to go now. I need to go." She nodded towards the door. Stef followed her eyes and saw the police walking in.

"Oh, right." He turned to Kevin. "Hey, listen, keep this all to yourself. At least until we figure it all out. OK?"

"Sure, I guess. But…" Kevin tried to stand but ended up further into the chair. Beatrice pulled him up, and he wrapped his arm around her waist. She pulled it away and nudged him to the door.

"Wait, where are we going?"

"Just keep walking," Stef urged Kevin, who was very drunk but could easily be pushed towards the direction he and Beatrice wanted him to go.

"Where are you taking me?" Kevin slurred. "Are you going to mug me?"

Stef laughed at him. Kevin joined him with giggles.

"Will you two stop with this shit?" Beatrice pulled them both through the arch at Porta Ticinese. She turned to Stef and slapped him.

"Ow!" He rubbed his cheek. "Beatrice, what are you doing?"

"This is not funny." She turned to Kevin. "Do you understand that we could be in danger?"

"Beatrice," Stef interrupted her.

"Stef, enough!"

"Beatrice, let's keep moving."

The threesome crossed the piazza and continued down the narrow Corso Ticinese, losing themselves in the crowd.

"Beatrice," Kevin tried to sound straight. "Are we in danger?"

"We can't really say—," Stef replied.

"Are you serious?" Beatrice stopped at the street crossing. "I was almost killed last night! And you can calmly say that?"

"You were almost killed?" Kevin's face turned white.

"Yes, I was almost killed. And the two of you better shape up or we could all be killed. Now keep moving." She crossed the street without waiting for them. She decided to keep the fast pace, or otherwise the drunk boys would slow them all down.

They held hands so as to not lose each other while weaving their way through the crowd of young people loitering around the columns of San Lorenzo.

"Where are we going?" Kevin shouted.

"I don't know," Stef replied and held Beatrice's arm. "Let's pop into a place and figure out what we're going to do."

"And at least tell me what the hell is going on?" Kevin said, trying to sound stern but those tiki drinks really hit him. "And maybe grab something to eat?"

Beatrice pulled them on the incoming tram and forced them both onto seats. She sat across from them glaring as the two men looked at each other and giggled.

CHAPTER 57

WHEN THE CAR door opened, he was pulled out and thrown to the ground. He felt a fist slam into his stomach and he keeled over.

"Fuck off!"

"Shut up." The man grabbed his right arm and pulled him away from the alley. "Keep quiet and stand up straight."

He was led around the corner, onto the main strip of the Gran Canal. The typically crowded area was uncharacteristically quiet. The few people walking down the strip quickened their pace upon seeing the two of them. They clearly appeared to look unsafe. He shook his arm from the man and ran. The man immediately pursued him. He could feel the man's attempt at grasping at him.

As he ran up the steps of the first footbridge, he felt the man grab his ankle. He fell to the ground, giving the man a good position to punch him over and over.

"Stop! Stop!" he whimpered. "Enough."

The man pulled him back to his feet and grabbed his throat.

"You run again, I will kill you." The man's breath reeked of onions.

He looked away and softened in defeat. The man pulled him back down the steps and along the canal. He shook his arm free again and climbed over the railing. The man grabbed him again and climbed the railing, holding his arm tight. He was pulled down onto one of the boats tied up along the canal wall. The man grabbed the back of his head and pushed into the water, holding his head under as he struggled to breathe.

CHAPTER 58

KEVIN CHEWED ON the rest of the pork bun as he retold his story to Beatrice. His mouth was full the whole time he spoke, but Beatrice looked past that to get the details he spilled in between bites. Stef glared at the noodles dangling from the chopsticks in his hand while he coaxed Kevin to continue with his story. Both men retold details in random order. Beatrice focused intently on piecing Kevin's incoherent timeline in order.

"So, let me understand this." She had had enough. She gave Stef a silent glare and took charge of the conversation. "Kevin."

"Yes," Kevin responded in mid bite. "Boy, these buns are delicious."

"Kevin, focus." Beatrice waved her hand in front of his face.

"Sorry, yes." He placed the other half of the second pork bun back down on the plate and looked her in the eye. "I'm listening."

"So you were in Paris—"

"Correct."

"And while you were there, a random fellow pick-pocketed you, stole your wallet."

"Well, he didn't pick-pocket me, really."

"How did he get your wallet?"

"I don't know, really." Kevin picked up the bun again. "I was on the train. And when I reached for my wallet – I don't remember why I was reaching for it then. Maybe to check the address? I'm not sure. Anyway, next thing I know, the wallet was gone."

"So the wallet was taken from you while you were on the train?" Beatrice kept repeating the details to get Kevin's story straight. It was a difficult task to do in his state of drunkenness, and while he was in the midst of gorging on the pork buns in front of him. She thought it was probably best to hold off until the protein hit his stomach and the inebriation subsided. Kevin reached for another bun, but instead picked up his warm tea.

"Kevin," Beatrice spoke softly and clearly. "You were on the train to Milan when you noticed your wallet was gone."

"Correct."

"Why were you coming to Milan, may I ask?"

Kevin didn't respond. Instead, he placed his tea cup back on the table and reached for the bowl of rice. He scooped the fried rice onto his plate, returned the bowl, and reached for the bok choy.

"Kevin." Beatrice focused on remaining calm. She had had enough of this drunk eating. But she knew he would be in a better state as he continued eating. In fact, she already noticed he was straightening up, not slurring, and had slowed his chewing to a normal pace.

"Sorry," Kevin finally responded, but this time it was after a complete swallow of the rice he had forked into his mouth. He was no longer talking with his mouth full – a good sign he was in a better state of mind. "I got to Milan and went directly to the police and told them about my wallet, and stuff."

"You went to the police?!" Stef and Beatrice said this in unison. They looked at each other and breathed.

"I mean, of course you went to the police." Stef portrayed a cool state.

"Yes, and I was dealing with all that for almost half the day."

"Well, that is pretty quick for Italy's standards," Stef retorted.

"But it seemed to take forever, really," Kevin continued. "I finally made it to my hotel, with no wallet, but at least I had my emergency credit card and my passport on me for identification. I always keep them separate when I travel. I was once advised to do that by a coworker that used to travel quite a lot. Anyway, I was able to check in for the night and I figured I'd sort out the wallet situation with my banks at home. So, that was my first night in Milan."

The server appeared with a steamer of dumplings and took away an empty bowl. He asked if everything was good and advised them that the rest would be coming out soon.

"What the hell did you guys order, the whole menu?" Beatrice commented even though she knew it had been a mistake to let the stupidly drunk men order their own food.

"I think we only have the scallion pancakes coming," Stef replied as he picked up a dumpling with his chopsticks. "Am I right, Kevin?"

"We ordered pancakes too?"

"OK, enough." Beatrice left the table and asked the server to cancel the rest of the order – which, she had found out, was two more orders of dumplings, one more of vegetable roll, and another noodle dish. Fortunately, the kitchen had not begun to cook any of it, so it was an easy cancellation; the staff obliged. She returned to the table and continued to get the rest of the timeline.

"OK, and wow." Beatrice looked at the new plate of dumplings. "They're already gone?" She adjusted her seat and took the remaining dumpling. "Kevin, you checked into the hotel. But you had mentioned you had an appointment?"

"Hmm?" Kevin sipped his water. "Oh, yes. I was supposed to meet someone at your bar."

"Who?" Stef and Beatrice asked together. Beatrice wished Stef would just shut the fuck up. She gave him a glare, and he understood.

"Well, that's a separate story, really."

"Maybe not," Beatrice pushed. "Let's get everything in order. This will help us figure out, maybe, what could be going on."

"Good point. So, back in Paris—"

"We're in Paris again?" Stef couldn't help himself. He was tired of this back and forth in his story. He wanted to take Kevin by the shoulders and shake the damn story out of him.

"Sorry." Kevin sat back.

"No, don't apologize." Beatrice rubbed his forearm. "We're here to help you. Let's figure this out."

"I'm sorry." Stef leaned in to Kevin. "I'm just confused. Please, continue."

"I met a man at a café," Kevin continued. "He sat next to me and asked me about the United States and the state of our politics. He seemed genuinely concerned about what's going on. Anyway, we got to talking, and I told him I was on a solo vacation, just to get away from life for a bit. You know, just a little escape."

"OK," Beatrice coaxed him further.

"Anyway, it was my last night at my hotel in Paris, and he asked where I was off to next on my adventure, and I told him I hadn't decided yet. I forgot to mention, I had just come from the Louvre, and the café was not far from there. He had asked me what I thought of the museum. Did I go see the *Mona Lisa*, what did I think of it? Anyway, when I told him I was impressed with Leonardo's work, he suggested I go to Milan. That I may be interested in seeing *The Last Supper*. Then he proceeded to tell me about Milan and the region. It was enough to make me consider coming here, so I decided I would. I thanked the man and went back to my hotel."

"So, this is why you came to Milan?" Beatrice repeated. "To see *The Last Supper*?"

"Well, yes, and no."

"There's more?"

"Yes." Kevin pushed his chair in. "The following day, I checked out of my hotel and took a taxi to the train station."

"Why did you not fly here?"

"Oh, I forgot to mention, the man suggested I take the new speed train. He had said something about seeing the views and it was a lovely experience. Well, he said 'easier' experience than going through security and boarding a flight and all that."

"That's what I say!" Stef added in excitement. "You see Beatrice, I always said flying takes away some adventure."

"Yes, Stef. You do say that." Beatrice rolled her eyes and looked back at Kevin. "Go on, Kevin. Please."

"Unfortunately, when I went to buy the ticket for the next train to Milan, there wasn't anything available until that evening. But I could get the train to Cannes and then switch over that night. So, that's what I purchased."

"So you stopped in Cannes?" Beatrice prodded.

"No."

"I don't understand."

"Let him finish, Beatrice," Stef said in a condescending tone. Beatrice wanted to slap him.

"As I left the ticket counter, I see the man from the bar!"

"Of course," Stef commented, then quickly kept to himself.

"He came up to me and greeted me, and asked me if I was going to Milan. I told him the situation with the ticket, and he kindly offered to talk to the ticket person for me. He went to the counter – he had asked me to wait where I was, near the bookshop – and returned and said he could possibly get me on that train. Of course I was interested."

"How would he get you on the train?" Beatrice asked.

"He said he could get the ticket but it was for special European courier service. And to take that spot, I would have to deliver the package that came with it."

"What?" Stef couldn't restrain himself. "You fell for that? People actually still fall for that?"

"What do you mean?" Kevin replied.

"He means nothing, Kevin," Beatrice talked over Stef. "So you took him up on the offer?"

"Well, yes. I mean, what would the harm be to deliver a package?"

"What would the harm be?" Stef repeated it. "Kevin, that could have been something illegal or worse, a weapon of some sort. How could you put yourself in that position?"

"Oh, of course it could have been that, but it wasn't. I saw the package. I saw the contents. It was harmless, really."

"What was it?" Beatrice spoke up hoping Stef would shut the fuck up.

"It was in the inside pocket of a blue blazer."

The words shot through Stef's memory like a bolt of lightning. He remembered it now. He remembered seeing Kevin on that train. He was the annoying American that sat across from him. He ran through that train trip over and over. He remembered the American plopping down on the seat across from him – it was Kevin. He remembered the American hanging the blue blazer on the hook near his face – it was a navy blue sports jacket, to be precise – and Stef admired it.

"So someone took the blazer from you?" Stef said absentmindedly.

"How did you know?" Kevin was surprised at Stef's question. "Did I mention that at the bar?"

"Well, yes," Stef responded. "I mean, of course. How else would I know that? It's not like I was on that train with you."

"Wait a minute!" Kevin stood up. "That's it! That's where I've seen you! You looked familiar to me, and I couldn't quite place it. That's where I saw you!"

"What are you talking about?" Stef pulled Kevin back down into his seat. "Sit down."

"When you sat at my table that first time we met at the bar, I thought you looked familiar to me," Kevin continued. "We met on the train."

"Kevin, you're drunk." Stef said the words hoping it would rationalize a confusion.

"No, I'm not." Kevin sat up and turned to Stef. "You just said you prefer train travel."

"So?"

"So?" Kevin slapped the table. "So, there's a chance you were on the same train from Paris to Milan. No?"

"Well, it is a possibility, Kevin, but—"

"What are the odds?" Kevin sat back in his seat, looking as if he had just solved a puzzle, and plopped a wonton cracker in his mouth.

"But," Stef continued. "I hadn't been on a train in months. So it was not me."

"But he looked like you," Kevin replied. "Well, resembled you and your...style. Your attitude."

"Attitude?"

"You know, that I'm-better-than-you snob attitude."

Beatrice chuckled at the comment.

"What are you laughing at, Bea?" Stef was offended.

"Nothing." Beatrice smiled at him and focused her attention back to Kevin. "Kevin, continue with your story, please. So you were on the train, blue jacket, which I assume you wore or hung on a hook?"

"Yes," Kevin replied after looking at Stef suspiciously. "And across from me was a man who resembled this guy over here."

Stef gave them both a side eye.

"Yes, attitude. Just like that," Kevin added, then continued. "I think I dozed off, and when I woke up, the jacket was gone."

"Of course it was," Stef mumbled, causing Beatrice to kick his shin. "Ouch!"

"I looked down the aisle and saw a man with the blue sports jacket, so I ran after him. Unfortunately, it wasn't my jacket, so that was a bit embarrassing. Anyway, I informed the conductor, that's when I noticed my wallet gone too!"

"Damn, you really were a good target," Stef added. He noticed Beatrice staring at him, then shut his mouth.

"And," Kevin continued, "when we got to the station, it took some time to finally talk to security."

"Of course it did." Stef couldn't control himself.

"Anyway, once they took my information, I went to my hotel. Now, I was supposed to drop the jacket at your bar when I arrived. However, being detained at the police station, and my wallet gone, delayed me. And I did not have the jacket."

"What was so special about this jacket?" Stef asked.

"Well, I'm not sure, really. The man told me it was left behind by his coworker, whom I was supposed to meet. It seemed legitimate, maybe…Anyway, I wrote down the meeting place, date, and time and placed it inside of the left pocket. Oh! That's when I discovered a something wrapped in a scarf. I opened it up and it was a bracelet and a shipping document!"

"Bracelet?!" Stef and Beatrice asked in unison, and immediately looked at each other.

Beatrice was in shock. The bracelet in question was in her coat pocket at that very moment. She debated whether she should reveal she had taken it from Elena's event. How could she tell them without appearing to be immature trying to enact some sort of revenge on Elena? Why would stealing her bracelet do anything anyway? She felt like a fool. She reached into her pocket and grasped the bracelet, but when she looked at Stef's concerned face, she left the bracelet in her pocket and kept silent.

Stef had figured it out. The bracelet was the item he was supposed to take in Berlin. The item he had failed to take, twice. So Flavio's man succeeded in taking the bracelet, and probably murdered the old woman while he was there. He probably did not expect her to be home, so he resorted to murder. Maybe? But then Kevin had the bracelet. But he couldn't possibly be the man Flavio had hired – he was too naive. That man in the river must have been Flavio's hire. Maybe? But how was Elena involved?

"Shipping document?" Stef repeated the words slowly. *Was this the connection to Elena?*

"Yes, the document was some sort of shipping receipt. But I don't quite remember. I didn't really pay attention to it. But I put the bracelet in my bag before hanging the jacket on the hook." Kevin pushed his plate away from the edge and leaned on the table. "I'm just confused here."

"About what, Kevin?"

"Well, I was supposed to meet this person at your bar, Beatrice."

"With the bracelet, yes?" Beatrice replied.

"And the shipping document. But I missed the appointment, as you know." Kevin rubbed his temples. "And from what Stef had mentioned, someone did come into the bar, posing as me, and he was later found dead somewhere."

"What?" Beatrice was shocked Kevin had even mentioned that. What had Stef told him?

"Yes, Beatrice," Stef chimed in. "I told Kevin about that man that had tried to use his credit card and was later found dead somewhere on the other side of town. Don't you remember? That was why we thought we knew this Kevin."

"Oh, right." Beatrice tried to look relieved, but she couldn't help but feel shaken inside. "Poor guy."

"Well," Kevin continued. "The man had clearly intended to make my appointment – he must have found the note in my wallet and maybe the shipping document – which I still don't understand why he would go to the appointment if he was the thief who actually had stolen the jacket."

"Kevin," Stef rolled his eyes. "I think…well, maybe, possibly, most likely, that man who had stolen your jacket on the train could be the same man who had given you the jacket in the first place?"

"What?"

"Let's say it's a possibility," Stef added.

"But, why?"

"I don't know." Stef gave up and sipped his water.

"So, why did you come to the bar the night you came?" Beatrice was determined to piece it all together.

"Oh, right." Kevin sat up again. "Well, I suppose I was curious. But also, I still had the bracelet. But the funny thing was what happened later that night."

"What happened later?" Beatrice asked.

"I received a note, at my hotel. Again, it had arrived a couple of days earlier, but I guess it was somehow misplaced."

"What do you mean?"

"The person at the desk, who recognized me, or thought she had recognized me, handed it to me."

"What are you talking about?" Beatrice asked.

"The first morning at the hotel." Kevin turned to Stef. "I told you this earlier. The person at the front desk wished me a good morning and asked if I wanted my belongings. I was confused and assumed it was some type of misunderstanding or language barrier thing. I just said, 'Thank you I already have my things,' and left for my morning walk."

"Yes?" Stef confirmed.

"When I returned from my walk, there was a different person at the front desk. And that person handed me the note with my key and apologized for not giving it to me earlier. 'There was a confusion with the room,' she said. I didn't know what she was talking about. In fact, I forgot about it until earlier when I told you."

"And that's what prompted you to come to the bar." Beatrice brought the story back on track.

"Correct." Kevin took a while to respond. His eyes were heavy. "I think I need to turn in."

"But Kevin," Stef prompted him. "We are getting close to figuring this out."

"Figuring what out?" Kevin replied after a long, drawn out yawn.

"You've just figured it out," Beatrice said to Stef. "The man who took his wallet was probably the same man who took the jacket with the shipping document. The same man came into my bar to meet with whomever, and as a result, he was…"

She couldn't finish her sentence. She wanted to forget that whole incident had ever happened. She wanted to forget that she was a participant in removing the body, in transporting the body, and in dumping the body. Hearing the words laid out like that reminded her it was all reality. It all happened, and it was all coming back to her, to them.

"Wait!" Stef said. "What about the bracelet?"

Beatrice turned red, looked down, and fiddled with a broken fortune cookie.

"Oh!" Kevin replied. "Well, I managed to succeed there. I gave it to Elena."

"What?"

"I happened to encounter her by Sant'Ambrogio," Kevin replied. "After leaving the bar that first night we met, I took the train and it happened to go in that direction. I had remembered the note in the envelope at the hotel had mentioned to meet Elena at some shop in Sant'Ambrogio – I was very late. Anyway, I was there and she was there – fixing her window display, fortunately. I told her I had a bracelet that I was supposed to deliver to her. It was back at my hotel. And so she asked me to deliver it at that event last night. Where I saw you, Stef."

A long silence crept up between the three of them. Beatrice was not going to share that she had the bracelet. She decided she would tell Stef after they left. She shuffled for her coat. Kevin rose from his seat. His exhaustion required him to balance himself, and he followed Stef and Beatrice out the door.

Without even a mention, Beatrice automatically followed Stef towards his apartment, which was conveniently located nearby. She had to tell him. And she still wanted his comfort. She didn't want to foolishly get intimate with Stef and would refuse if he were to attempt anything. She immediately decided his apartment would not be a good idea.

"Where are you going?" She stopped.

"Back to my place," Stef replied. "It's late."

"Well," Kevin interrupted. "I'm going to get a taxi back to my hotel."

"Yes, and I'm going to get a taxi too." Beatrice hooked under Kevin's arm. "Stef, can you accompany me back to the bar."

"Beatrice," Stef pleaded.

"Come with me," she suggested to Stef.

"Oh, alright."

When they reached piazza Moscova, Kevin crawled into the first taxi they spotted. Beatrice and Stef kept on walking until they found another.

Chapter **59**

KEVIN STUMBLED OUT of the taxi and straightened himself before entering the small lobby at his hotel. He was no longer drunk, but the exhaustion made him feel that way. He walked up to the young man behind the counter and asked for his key.

"Yes sir," the boy replied with a very thick accent. "Name, please."

"Benton, Kevin. Room 21."

"Benton," the boy repeated and looked at the computer register. He typed and fooled around with the mouse for some time then looked up again with a puzzled face. "Ah, here it is. Sorry."

The boy turned around, grabbed the key hanging from number 17, and handed it to Kevin.

"Oh, wait," Kevin looked at the key. "I'm Room 21. My key is hanging right there. You gave me the wrong key."

"I'm sorry, sir?"

"I'm Room 21."

"Benton, Kevin. No?"

"Yes."

"Room 17. That is what I have here."

"Well, that's incorrect. I'm room 21. Two. One."

"Oh, yes. Two. One," the boy repeated and handed him the correct key. He turned to hang the other key back on number 17 and added, "Will your guest be returning today?"

"My guest?"

"Yes. In room 17."

"I don't have a guest. I have nothing to do with Room 17."

The boy looked at his screen again, clearly perplexed. He picked up the phone and talked to the person on the other end. The door behind the boy opened, and an older man walked out. They both looked at the screen and back up at Kevin.

"Sir," said the older man. "I'm sorry for the confusion. We seem to have your name listed on two rooms."

Chapter 60

STEF FLUSHED THE urinal and turned the faucet on to wash his hands. He struggled pushing the soap out of the dispenser. *Damn drunks*, he thought to himself, *keep breaking this thing*. He had told Beatrice to get it fixed a while ago, but she repeated that the bar owner kept putting it off.

He looked at his reflection in the mirror. He hadn't stopped to examine his face in a long time. But at that moment he got lost in it. The age was not showing as much as he had thought. Maybe it was the lighting. He noticed a pimple forming on his right cheek. He used his wet fingers and squeezed on it to no avail. It only made the area red and sore.

A sudden feeling of rejection came over him, fueled by Elena's indifference toward him. He hated that she had this power over his feelings. She was never available emotionally, and she never would be. Although Paolo did stray now and then, Elena had committed to stay with him. He was always there and would always be. Stef knew it. He knew that there would never be a space for him in Elena's life. Well, the only space she would give him was the side of the bed Paolo left empty when he was away or with another.

He turned off the faucet, dried his hands, and looked at his face again. His hair looked dry and ratty. He couldn't remember the last time he had washed it. Apparently, he hadn't been focusing on his appearance lately, not as much as he used to. Is that what happens when you get older? He stepped back and examined his torso; his waist was still firm and sexy.

Stef looked again and noticed reflections of wet footprints on the tiled floor. The footsteps led to the vestibule behind him. He pushed open the door to a frightened and familiar looking man standing on the toilet, hair wet, finger to his lips, signaling a plea for Stef to be silent. Stef looked at him with confusion, but remained quiet. The man had a familiar face. The wet face, the wet hair. At first, he thought it was Kevin, then realized the man standing before him was the man that he had previously found dead on that bathroom floor; the man in the river.

"How is this possible?" he whispered aloud. He stood frozen in shock.

The familiar stranger put his finger back up to his lips, stretched his other arm to reveal a gun, and mouthed the words 'Help Me'.

Beatrice poured herself a whiskey, lit a cigarette, and waited for Stef to return from the bathroom. She took a shot of whiskey when she heard the door open, reminding her that she had not locked it behind her.

She looked up and saw Kevin standing at the entrance with an oversized plastic bag. When they had separated, Kevin had agreed to go back to the hotel. Apparently, Kevin had discovered something, and he seemed very nervous about whatever he had inside of the bag.

"You startled me, Kevin."

Kevin did not reply. He walked slowly towards Beatrice and placed the bag onto the bar.

"What have you got there?" Beatrice said looking into his worrisome eyes.

"You would not believe it," Kevin replied. "It's the missing blazer."

Chapter 61

A LOUD BANG was heard from the bathroom in back. Both Kevin and Beatrice jumped in terror.

"Stef!" she called out, trembling. "Stef, are you OK? Can you come out here please?"

"Stef?" Kevin repeated. "I'll go check on him." Kevin disappeared into the back area, toward the bathroom doors.

Beatrice examined the blazer. Whomever had the blazer was searching for something inside of it. Her examination was interrupted by a loud bump from the back office. She walked over to the bathroom, passed the kitchen door, and suddenly felt a hand cover her mouth.

"Don't make a sound," growled the voice of a strange man. She felt a gun pressed to her back. "I know what you did. And I'm not happy about it."

Beatrice breathed heavily; her heart was racing.

"He was an asshole, sure. But he didn't deserve to die like that."

She began to tremble. This man was clearly connected to the man that chased her, the man that fell in the Galleria. He was going to kill her! He pulled her in tightly and continued to talk.

"I'm going to make this really easy for you. I'm going to ask you a question, and you're going to answer directly and quietly. You understand me?"

Beatrice nodded. She could feel her heart throbbing with fear. She looked around for Kevin but did not find him.

"I'm going to let go of you," the man whispered as he led her back to the bar. "You're going to turn around and speak. OK?"

Beatrice nodded.

"Quietly. Slowly. Clearly. I'm going to let you go. All you have to do is tell me where you hid it." The man pulled away his gun, then pulled his hand away from her mouth.

Beatrice turned around and looked at the man but did not speak. She stood still, looking around the room for Kevin, but he was nowhere in sight. She examined the strange man. He had a grey sweater, black pants, and boots. She noticed his rugged build and immediately calculated what she could do to tackle him. He put his gun on the bar and leaned on the stool beside him. A scar angled on his left eyebrow looked almost like a decoration. His piercing eyes narrowed.

"You're going to tell me," the man said. "No games. I should add that I've been instructed to throw you in the canal out there. But I thought I'd do things a little differently here. And give you a chance to redeem yourself."

She was about to let out a scream, but another loud bang from the bathroom interrupted them.

Distracted, the man fell victim to Beatrice's kick to his head, knocking him to the ground. She attempted to grab his gun on the bar, but the man pulled her leg, causing her to accidently push the gun into the sink. The banging from the bathroom grew louder. Beatrice shook the man from her and ran to the bathroom. The man stumbled in pursuit.

"Stef, there's a man!" Beatrice slammed the door behind her, trying to find a lock. "Stef, help!"

"Beatrice...," Stef said softly.

"Get over here!"

"Beatrice, stop." Stef said it plainly. She was taken back by his reserved tone. She turned around and saw a man pointing a gun at him. The man looked familiar, but she couldn't place where she had seen him. Kevin was knocked out cold in the corner.

The door flung open; the burly man rushed in. He looked at all three of them and smiled. "Well, well, Stef. So, you have been hiding something from us, haven't you?"

"What?" Beatrice looked back and forth at all of them. "You know each other?"

"Yes, we know each other." The burly man signaled to his buddy to lower the gun. "I've got this, pinhead."

"What's going on here?" Stef finally spoke up and asked the burly man. "Who is this guy?"

"You don't recognize him?" The burly man laughed.

"Stef, what's going on here?" Beatrice kept her eyes on the man that followed her inside. She then looked at the wet man who held the gun to Stef, trying to place him. "How do I know you?"

The stranger was about to reply when the burly man interrupted. "You don't recognize him either?"

"Leave her out of this," Stef said with conviction. He wanted to protect Beatrice from all of it. He had to think of a way to get her out. "Let her go, and we can sort this all out."

"Let her go?" the wet stranger finally spoke. "Let her go? Ha!"

"She's not going anywhere," the burly man added.

"She has nothing to do with this." Stef took a step forward.

"Nothing to do with this?" the wet man laughed again. "Do you hear him, Luca? Nothing to do with this."

"Stop laughing," the burly Luca replied.

"No! I'm not going to stop laughing!" The wet man seethed. "I'm tired of this shit! After all I went through over all of this!"

"We've come to the end now," Luca tried quieting the stranger. "Keep your cool, and we'll get to it."

"Fuck off!" The stranger grabbed Beatrice. "Where is it?! Where is it?!"

"Let go of her!" Stef shouted.

"Why don't you shut the fuck up?" the stranger replied and then turned back to Beatrice. "Tell me where you put it."

"I don't know what you're talking about."

"I saw you," the stranger seethed. "At the party. You were in that room. You sat at the vanity, opened the wooden box, and took it. I saw you!"

Beatrice shook her head. He was in that dark room? How had she not seen him? The contents in that box were a silk scarf and the bronze bracelet. She had taken them. She had tied her hair up with the scarf and wore the bracelet. And he was watching her the entire time. The thought horrified her.

"The bracelet..." She said the word as she thought about his watching her.

"Yes...," the stranger said. "Where is it?"

Beatrice remembered the man had chased her through the fog. Was he after the bracelet? She shook her head.

The stranger slapped her left cheek with his back hand. Stef had had enough. He lunged at the stranger and pushed him against the sinks.

"Hey, stop it!" Luca shouted. He grabbed Stef and threw him against the stalls.

The stranger struggled to regain his balance. He stood up straight, looked around, and dropped to the floor, knocked out cold.

Luca had tried grabbing him, but Beatrice had taken her opportunity to kick the burly man in the groin and elbow his face when he keeled over. His heavy body fell backwards, hitting his head against the door. Luca then tried reaching for his gun, but Stef had gotten to it first.

"How about you tell me what the hell is going on?" he said as he waved the gun, signaling for the burly man to stand up.

Kevin groaned in the corner. Beatrice ran over and helped him stand.

"Kevin, are you OK?"

"Yeah," Kevin slurred. "I think so. My head hurts."

"Beatrice," Stef added. "Got any rope?"

"Rope?!" Luca exclaimed.

"I'm sure I've got something." Beatrice held Kevin's arm. "Come on," she said while leading him out of the bathroom.

"Don't call the police!" Luca pleaded. "Don't get them involved."

"Relax," Stef scoffed. "We're not stupid enough to do that."

Beatrice immediately returned with wires. "This is all I could find."

"That's fine." Stef took them from her and handed her the gun. "Hold it steady while I tie these guys up."

"Don't be an idiot," Luca laughed at him. "I have an idea."

"What's that?"

"Let's take him out of the equation." Luca gestured to the wet stranger knocked out on the floor.

"What?"

"We'll take him out of here and drop him somewhere. He's useless. Then you can go bring that thing to Flavio."

"Interesting suggestion," Stef replied. "How about we drop you someplace and we take him?"

"Oh really?" Luca laughed. "Where are you going to drop me?"

"How about in Piazza Duomo, just like your friend?" Beatrice surprised herself when she said it. She shook any look of surprise from her face, then added, "More than one bird can fly, you know. We can surely make you the second."

"Are you some crazy killer bitch?" Luca retorted and turned to Stef. "Who is this?"

"Put your hands behind your back, then we can talk."

Luca rolled his eyes and followed orders. Stef tied his wrists tight, looked him in the eyes, and slapped him.

"What the fuck?" Luca shouted.

"That's for Flavio. I've had enough of your shit," Stef replied and then turned to check the stranger. "Shit."

"What?" Beatrice and Luca said it together in unison.

Stef sat on the floor, rubbed his forehead, and said, "He's dead."

They all stared at him while he repeated it, then added, "For real this time."

Chapter 62

KEVIN LAY IN the back of the tram rubbing his head, still pounding from the blow. Beatrice leaned over the seat and wiped his forehead with a damp cloth.

"Are you OK, buddy?" Stef asked from across the aisle.

"Yeah," Kevin groaned. "I'll be OK. I'll be fine."

"Don't sit up." Beatrice held onto his arm. "Just relax."

"Where are we going?"

"Well, we wanted to leave Luca to do what Luca does. So, I figured we leave the area." Stef couldn't tell if Kevin was even listening to him. He added gesturing around the empty tram, "No taxis in sight, so…We'll go back to my place or something."

Kevin ignored Stef. He had caught a glimpse of the Castello Sforzesco out the window. Currently covered in scaffolding for maintenance, the castle, once a fortress built by the Duke Sforza of Milan, was now a museum and the south entrance to the grand Parco Sempione. Kevin adored museums. *That would be a good spot*, he thought. The tram slowed down to its final stop in piazza Cordusio. Kevin followed Stef and Beatrice off the vehicle.

"I'm OK," Kevin said to Beatrice, gently removing her arm from under his.

"You sure, Kevin?" Stef asked.

"Yes, I can walk. I'm good."

"OK, it's a bit far from here, but we're here to help you."

"I think I can manage, thank you," Kevin replied, shuffling behind the pair as they walked east towards the Brera.

He followed along listening to Stef coddle Beatrice, telling her everything was going to be fine.

But, what is? he thought. *What have I gotten myself into? None of this was part of the plan. I should have just stuck with my own mission and fuck them all. Fuck that man that offered me a ticket in Paris. Fuck these two who clearly want to keep me involved in whatever they are involved in. Who are they, anyway? Are they going to kill me? Why am I following them?*

"Kevin!" He heard Beatrice calling out to him as he ran to the castle entrance. "Kevin, where are you going? Kevin!"

"Is he still not well?" Stef asked Beatrice as the pair pursued Kevin.

"No. I mean, he's fine. But, this is not the pain. I think something else is going on with him."

"Kevin!" Stef called out to him. "Kevin, where did you go?"

The park was dark, save for lamplight scattered around the main opening and along the paths throughout. They searched for Kevin to no avail. He clearly wanted to rid himself of them. Beatrice couldn't blame him. After all, the poor guy was pulled into this mess and had no idea what he had gotten into.

"Where the hell could he have gone?" Stef spoke out to the emptiness. He rubbed his forehead with concern for what Kevin may do. *Will he run to the police? Where is he going?* "You don't think he'd go to the police, do you?"

Beatrice burst into sobs and dug her head into Stef's shoulder. Stef caressed her head.

"There, there." He embraced her. "Come on. No use standing here. He clearly wants to be alone."

"What if he does something?" Beatrice asked as she wiped her tears.

"All we can do now is hope he just sleeps on it and come to his senses," Stef replied, not realizing what Beatrice was really asking him.

Chapter 63

STEF SAT ON his couch waiting for Beatrice to make eye contact. She sat across from him on his oversized leather chair. She had reached into her pocket and placed the bracelet on his coffee table.

After explaining how she got the bracelet, she reverted back to silence, ignoring his questions.

"Let me get you a drink," Stef finally spoke again. "Water? Juice?"

Beatrice didn't respond. She continued staring out the window, rubbing her tears.

"I think an amaro would be good," Stef suggested. "I'll be right back."

Beatrice replied with a nod.

They sat across from each other silently sipping amaro until Beatrice finally spoke again.

"Stef?" She did not look up from her drink.

"Yes, Bea."

"There's something that still confuses me about this whole situation. And it hadn't even occurred to me until a few moments ago."

"What's that?" Stef leaned in.

"Well, we know now that Kevin is really Kevin – the man whose wallet we found."

"Yes?"

"Well, then who was that first guy? That stranger in the bathroom?"

"An imposter?"

"Yes, the fake Kevin. The one—" She leaned in and whispered, "The one that, you know, in the river. The one that died, again tonight, in the bathroom? And by the way, how *did* that Luca guy remove him? Clean it all up?"

"I don't know." Stef sipped his amaro. "I never ask the details. They just have their way. There was no big mess, though, really. No one will notice. They never do. Maybe a broken glass or so, but no one ever suspects anything."

Beatrice finished her amaro and finally looked at him. Stef looked away and breathed out. He hated that Beatrice, too, had been roped into the mess.

"Clearly, the stranger was a no one," Stef broke the silence. "In the end, he was nothing but a mistake. He was given a job and couldn't even complete it. Well, he made a mess of it all. He was just one big irrelevant mistake."

"Stef," Beatrice said his name softly as if she didn't want to say what followed. "I think we need to end this."

"What?" Stef awoke from his thoughts.

"This whatever this is. I can't do this anymore. I need to be away from you."

The words hit him like an anvil to his ego. Beatrice was cutting him off. He wanted to say something, but he was too surprised to even think of what he could say.

"I think I'm going to leave for a little while," Beatrice continued.

"Where are you going?"

"I don't know yet. I just need to get away. Maybe Tuscany. I don't know."

"Alone? Can you handle that?" Stef blurted the question before he could even stop himself. Instantly, he saw in Beatrice that the question was not received well.

"That is none of your concern," she replied, then faced the door and turned the handle. "I'm going to go now. We're done here." She opened the door, but stopped herself at the threshold. She turned back to Stef and slapped him as hard as she could muster. Stef stood in pain, watching her walk out the door, then dropped back down on the couch and silently rubbed his stinging left cheek.

Chapter 64

KEVIN WATCHED THE pair shuffle out of the park and down the street away from him, without a care. It was confirmation that the two of them did not care about him nor what was to become of him. They used him too. They just wanted information from him. They didn't give a shit about him. He gathered his thoughts and faced reality: *Well, why would they care about me? They hardly even know me. I can't blame them. They don't know what I'm feeling, what I'm thinking. Do they?* It didn't matter.

He continued to climb up the scaffold along the left side of the fortress's main tower. He stepped off the scaffold and onto the outer ledge of the tower's top tier. He looked across the dark park and the randomly placed glow of lampposts scattered about. He then looked down to the pavement and whimpered.

Is this going to be it? The way I should do it? A sudden sense of dizziness come over him. It had been years since he climbed anything; the experience of vertigo had put a stop to that. *Don't look down*, he thought. He looked up at the landscape of the city lights to his left, then to his right.

He took a deep breath and leaned out towards the ground, balancing himself away from the tower wall.

Immediately, he leaned back against the wall again, second guessing his actions. He took two side steps back towards the scaffold.

"No," he said aloud. But he wasn't telling himself not to jump. He was telling himself not to chicken out. "No one needs me," he reminded himself. "No one ever needed me. It's for the best. It's what I came to do."

He looked down, smiled a sad smile, and stepped off the ledge.

CHAPTER 65

IT HAD BEEN years since he ever felt his body tremble like it was at that moment. He stared into the hospital room looking at Kevin's motionless body lying dressed in a hospital gown, bandages on the left of his face. He was in a state of deep sleep.

Stef did not want to believe that Kevin had considered ending his life. That he had planned his whole European trip around finding a place to just put an end to it all.

He just didn't want to believe it was possible. He didn't believe it until he saw the news coverage of a man found badly hurt at the foot of the Castello. He had come in from the kitchen and listened to the morning news as usual, when he heard the newswoman describe the horrible scene.

"The man seemed to have appeared to have fallen from the top of the tower of the Castello Sforzesco, however police could not confirm nor deny that was the case."

The camera had zoomed in to the scene and showed Kevin out cold onto a stretcher. Stef dropped his espresso cup and fell onto his knees and sobbed. He didn't know why he cried for Kevin, after all, he barely knew him. But he cried, and he cried a lot.

How could someone get to that point in their life? Stef thought to himself as he stared through the window.

"Twenty stitches to the side of his face," the nurse stated this fact before Stef had asked. Stef remained silent and continued to look into the room.

"Sir," the nurse continued." Are you a relative?"

"Sure," Stef nodded, turned away from Kevin's room, and exited the ward before the nurse had a chance to continue her questioning.

Chapter 66

"**ARE YOU REALLY** going to eat all that?" Stef said while staring at the oversized veal cutlet hanging over the plate.

"Of course I am," Flavio replied. "This is a classic *costoletta alla Milanese*."

"It's fucking huge."

"Well, that's why they call it *l'orecchia di elefante*," Flavio responded, annoyed. "And yes, I'm going to eat it all. It's part of my diet. Is that better?"

Stef raised his eyebrow and sipped his prosecco.

"So," he continued. "You thought your new guy never took the bracelet out of the apartment?"

"Apparently," Flavio replied. "The douche went rogue. When my guys found him by the river – yes, I had them follow you two fools – he told us he never got the bracelet. Instead, he ended up being caught by surprise and so he killed the old woman that lived there."

"Why didn't you say anything to me?" Stef filled his glass.

"Because I wanted you to find that dumb American." Flavio took his first bite and chewed for a while before continuing. "When I was told the American had the bracelet, I thought you would be the best guy for the job."

Stef looked at him.

"OK," Flavio added. "At first, I did think you were involved in it. But, after talking with you I believed that you weren't. So, I figured I'd get my money's worth and have you do something else for me. And you managed to even fuck that one up."

"You've got the bracelet," Stef retorted.

"Yes, but I lost a guy in the whole process."

"That was his own fault."

Flavio shook his head, looked back down at his *costoletta*, and sliced off another bite.

"How did Elena get involved?" Stef pushed him for more.

"Naturally—" Flavio took another sip and continued, "We had to find another way to get the item, and quick. When we heard the furniture was up for auction, I was instructed to find someone to purchase the furniture pieces, most importantly the wooden box. Which, at the time, I still thought contained the bracelet. And so I remembered you had once mentioned this friend that was in the furniture business…So, I thought I would employ her."

"Why would you get her involved?" Stef slammed his fist on the table.

"Relax, she had no idea what was going on." Flavio ordered a second glass of wine. "I didn't tell her I knew you. I just mentioned the opportunity and that she would be able to get some pieces for herself. It was a great deal."

Stef breathed out and held his face in his hands.

"Your friend Elena had no idea why she was hired," Flavio explained. "Or who even hired me to hire her. But she was told to purchase specific pieces. When the pieces were moved out of the home and into the shipping container, our men – working for the moving company – included the wooden box and its contents, as instructed. Apparently, our foolish friend did do something right – he hid the box inside of the couch. Even though the bastard took the contents – asshole. Anyway, that turned out to be the easiest way to steal the piece. If anyone had been searching for it, they never would suspect it was in that shipment. Even though it was never in the shipment.

"When the shipment was to arrive," Flavio continued, "Elena had been instructed to take specific small items out and put them in a safe place immediately. This was so in case Interpol or anyone had caught up with shipment to check for the lost item, Elena would have already taken the box out of the shipment. She had followed instructions, but there was no Interpol or customs check anyway. This was all unbeknownst to her, of course. I intended to keep her safe. I didn't want her to know anything."

"This is a fucking mess." Stef shot down his Prosecco. "Is she in danger?"

"No. I promise she is in no danger. Especially now that you brought it to me."

"What is it with this bracelet, anyway?"

"You don't need to know that." Flavio returned his napkin onto his lap. "My food is getting cold. Are you sure I can't offer you anything?"

"No, I'll just take my money."

Flavio pushed the envelope to Stef. When Stef grabbed for it, Flavio put his hand on his.

"How about another job, Stef?"

Chapter 67

THE IMAGE OF Beatrice walking away from him ran through his mind over and over. What could he have done differently? If only he had not gotten her involved in the whole mess. It wasn't fair to have her accompany him in removing fake-Kevin's body that night. He didn't need her. He was just selfish and wanted to have a hold on her to avoid her from going to the police. He didn't think about her safety or well-being. He was selfish. She didn't deserve any of it. And he didn't deserve her.

He should have let her stay out of his life, but he couldn't. Deep down, it bothered him that she wasn't around anymore. That she didn't want to be in his life. He kept going back to her. He wanted her. He wanted to be the man she needed. He knew she didn't need him, but he wanted to be that man for her. Being around her, with her, reminded him of the man he used to be, or rather the man he could have been. The man that he was not. And now she was gone. He rested his head on the window with his thoughts, bringing him to tears again.

Poor Kevin, he thought. He managed to insert himself in all of this, not realizing the potential consequences. The man was naïve, but there was something about him. Whatever he had been going through, it frightened Stef to see a man resort to such a drastic decision.

And Elena. He hadn't even fully processed Elena's involvement in all of it. He had already been feeling the effects of losing her social connections, of not being in her life romantically, and she made it clear she never had any intention for him other than the occasional bedroom romp.

He felt the train lean slightly to the right as the track curved further south towards Rome. He looked out the window and imagined what his life would be now. No more social champagne gatherings with Elena's group. No more smooth entries to exclusive clubs or restaurants; not without Elena or her connections.

His age hindered his attempts at reviving his escorting. His lack of patience hindered his attempts at returning to thievery. His failure to secure any odd jobs further hindered his income stream. He knew he had to eventually let go of his downgraded plush apartment in Brera. He didn't know what to do. He felt a sudden sense of uselessness. He banked all of his steps forward using his handsome looks and charm, but those weren't opening as many doors as they used to. What was he to become?

He felt the tears filling up his eyes. He leaned heavier on the window and stared at the countryside passing by. A teardrop trickled down his left cheek.

The train slowly made its way into Termini station, binario twelve. Just a layover until it continued its journey south towards Naples. As the train bumped to a stop, Stef thought of just not moving forward. He could stop and end the sham of a life into which he had again fallen. He grabbed his olive green leather weekender bag and stepped off the train. He didn't know where he was going to go. He was back in Rome. Part of him wanted to see Patrizia again. Would she want to see him after all of these years?

He stepped off the tram and walked down the narrow cobblestone street towards where the Cin Cin bar once stood. As he approached the double glass doors, he was reminded that the once bopping jazz bar had been turned into a modern osteria. Any reminder of the Cin Cin was gone. She was gone. From the doorway, he stared at the door to the back kitchen and reminisced about the last time he had seen Patrizia.

It was many years ago. He had been wandering around Trastevere, just as he was now, crying over both Beatrice and Patrizia. Beatrice had told him she was tired of being second fiddle to her coworker. She had given him an ultimatum: tell Patrizia, end it with Patrizia, and be with her. But he couldn't bring himself to do it.

The memory of one horrible night back then had popped into his mind.

/ / /

He was walking the area and had stopped on a bench by the Tiber, swigging from a bottle of whiskey, sobbing like a little boy. He was ashamed of himself. *Why can I not remain faithful to one person?* Patrizia was good for him, and he knew it. But after she had ended it with him, he couldn't bring himself to be with Beatrice because he still wanted Patrizia. He had then pulled himself together, stood up from the bench, and stumbled into the Cin Cin bar that dreadful night.

He remembered it was late, the jazz music that the bar was known for was blaring. He was determined to go in inconspicuously so as to not cause a scene with her. He entered through the front entrance, camouflaging himself in a group of patrons. Once they passed that annoying mime server, he broke away and plopped down into an oversized green armchair situated by the back corner. The mime appeared on Stef's right side.

"Stef," He said his name with surprise. "I didn't see you walk in."

"Aurelio," Stef leaned in with a low voice. "No one knows I'm here. Please keep it to yourself. A whiskey and soda, please."

"Sure, no problem." Aurelio replied, flung his cape, and disappeared into the crowd.

Stef had sat in the chair for almost an hour, drinking more whiskey and sodas than he probably should have. He kept scanning the room for Patrizia. He almost gave up on his quest until she appeared from the back kitchen. He watched her unnoticed as she pulled a man in from behind her. It was that American man, his face bandaged up. Apparently Stef wasn't the only one who wanted to kick his ass. Stef sipped his whiskey and soda, watching as the pair sat on a couch talking and exchanging occasional caresses.

He watched as Patrizia pulled out her deck of cards, probably showing the American one of her typical card tricks; something guaranteed to generate a laugh. Water filled his eyes again. It was torture watching a girl he wanted to love possibly falling for another man. He swallowed the rest of his whiskey and soda, then picked up the next glass Aurelio had snuck onto his table. He sulked in the chair and continued to watch Patrizia and the American. The pair had moved in very closely together, lowered themselves onto the couch, and engaged in a passionate kiss.

His eyes would not recover; he could barely see them through the tears. He gulped the whiskey and soda and rushed out the door, pushing passed Aurelio who was trying to say goodbye. Stef ignored him and stormed out, back to the Tiber. He dropped down on the river walk and sobbed.

/ / /

It was now years later and there he was again in Rome, standing in the doorway of the former bar. The memories of that last moment he saw Patrizia still continued to haunt him. He turned away with tears in his eyes, and took a taxi back to Termini station.

He walked down the platform of the train station, crying. He felt a heavy sense of sadness come over him. He was alone. He was useless. He was a nothing. He wanted to believe it would get better, but he didn't believe it.

His train had left the station, continuing south to Naples. He continued walking until he reached the end of the platform. He stared at the web of the train tracks ahead of him.

He jumped off the platform and walked along the track, not even thinking to see if anyone was trying to stop him. He just kept walking. He swung his leather bag back and forth as he continued, almost automatically, down the track. His eyes filled up again, and he sobbed.

He heard a train coming in towards him. He didn't even know if he was in the way; he didn't care. He just stared at the train – unsure if it was on the same track at all – wondering if he should do it. Was he ready to end it? *Is this what Kevin was feeling?* Unsure of himself, he reached into his right inside pocket and wove his fingers into the folds of the silk scarf. In an instant, he smiled, caressing the bronze bracelet wrapped inside.

# # #

AUTHOR'S NOTE

I personally consider part of this story as my contribution to the discussion on mental illness and depression. In researching this novel, I read a lot about depression and loneliness in both men and women and spoke to people in my life who are struggling with this personal affliction.

Depression is a silent torturer that many people experience in life, if not often, at least at some point. Sometimes the feeling gets a strong hold on someone and that takes us all by surprise, resulting in us asking ourselves: how did we not know?

If you or someone you know has recurrent feelings of depression and loneliness, please don't be ashamed. Please talk and listen. Many of us are out there to love, understand, listen, and help. Talk to someone you know, or reach out to the many services that are out there to help.

But, most of all:

Do Not Feel Ashamed.

Talk. Listen. Understand. Love.

CPSIA information can be obtained
at www.ICGtesting.com
Printed in the USA
BVHW080758301120
594467BV00003B/107